PLANTED
—— FOR A ——
PURPOSE

Craig Minty

PLANTED FOR A PURPOSE

by Craig Minty

Copyright © 2025 Craig Minty

All rights reserved.

No part of this publication may be reproduced, stored in a retrieval system, or transmitted in any form or by any means—electronic, mechanical, photocopy, recording or otherwise—without the prior written permission of the author, except in the case of brief quotations embodied in critical articles or reviews.

Scripture quotations are taken from the New King James Version®. Copyright © 1982 by Thomas Nelson. Used by permission. All rights reserved.

This is a work of fiction inspired by Biblical accounts and ancient cultural contexts. While rooted in Scripture, particularly the Gospel narratives, many characters, events, and conversations have been imaginatively developed to enrich the story.

Names, places, and incidents not found directly in the Bible are either products of the author's imagination or are used fictitiously. This book is not intended as a theological or historical commentary, but as a creative and reflective retelling grounded in the truth of God's Word.

First Edition

Edited by Kimberly Mary

Cover design by Marigold Emal

Interior design and layout by Judy Sery – Sparrow Publishing

Published in Australia by Saved by Grace Stories

ISBN: 978-1-7641519-2-4 (Paperback)
ISBN: 978-1-7641519-3-1 (Kindle eBook)

Printed and distributed via Amazon KDP

www.amazon.com/author/craigminty

Dedication

To my Heavenly Father, this book is first and foremost Yours.

The stories You place on my heart—stories of grace, peace, and love—often leave me at a loss for words. Still, You let me write them.

May I never bury the talents You give, but offer what little I have for Your glory.

To my friend Hila, on whom the character within this novel is dedicated.

הקדשה

אני מתפלל לשלום ישראל, ושתחוש את אהבת אלוהים.
דרך הספר הזה, מי ייתן ולעולם לא תרגיש שנשכחת,
שתמיד תרגיש אהוב, ושתדע שהוא נאמן.

Preface

Bible stories are such wonderful stories

Some of my earliest and fondest memories are of hearing about incredible feats—Joshua and the battle of Jericho, Jonah and the whale (which, many years later, I discovered was actually a "big fish"), David and Goliath, Noah and the Ark, Moses parting the Red Sea, Ruth, and Esther. Then there was Jesus walking on water, and feeding five thousand with a boy's small lunch, and healing the blind man by spitting on the ground to create mud, and restoring the cripple at the pool, and cleansing the forgotten lepers, and turning tables in the temple, and giving Bartimeus sight, and the woman at the well, and well, the stories about Jesus keep coming.

Then there was Paul—fearless and tireless, preaching across continents—and Peter, brimming with boldness, stumbling and standing again. And Samuel, just a boy, hearing God's voice in the quiet hours of the night. The list could go on and on.

These weren't just stories read aloud in hushed voices—they were *given* to me, like heirlooms wrapped in love. Passed down from my grandmother, my mum, my Sunday School teacher, and many others whose voices still echo in my memory. And as I grew older, what began as something handed to me became something I pursued.

The Bible—and the study of it—became more than a Sunday habit; it became a quiet passion, a lifelong pursuit. A hobby, yes—but one that never grew old. These weren't merely stories *about* people. They became stories that shaped *me*. Stories I would return to again and again, finding something new each time, like light shifting through stained glass.

But it wasn't until a particular Sunday morning at my home church—LifeHouse Church—that something shifted. Pastor Richard Kobakian was preaching, as he so often does, with fire in his voice and truth in his eyes. In the middle of one of his soul-stirring sermons, he mentioned a familiar character: Zacchaeus.

Now, perhaps Zacchaeus always felt like a kindred spirit to me. You see, I didn't exactly "grow up"—at least not at first. For many years, I was the shortest student in my year level. I was the one who had to stand at the front of every photo, the one who craned his neck in assemblies, who was more likely to see shoulders than stages. So Zacchaeus, I get it. I really do.

But then Ps. Richard posed a question I'd never thought to ask. While retelling the familiar story of Zacchaeus climbing the sycamore tree to catch a glimpse of Jesus, he paused and said:

"Who planted the tree?"

It was a passing comment—barely a line in a sermon rich with insight—but for me, it was the seed of something far deeper. That question took root. And from it, this story began to grow.

So, thank you, Pastor Richard, for that moment of wonder.

And to you, dear reader—yes, consider this your *spoiler alert*. You've already glimpsed the heart of this book: a tree, planted for a purpose. But this story isn't just about that tree. It's about how it came to be—how, in one of the world's oldest continually inhabited cities, a simple act of obedience bore fruit generations later in one of the most profound moments in the Gospels.

Because sometimes, before there's a miracle, there's a moment no one notices.

Before Zacchaeus climbed, someone dug. Someone planted. Someone believed.

And in our fast-paced, content-saturated world, we seem to have lost the art and the importance of telling stories. You see, stories still hold power. I've seen it time and time again in classrooms full of jostling students—restless, distracted, half-listening. Then I say five simple words:

"Let me tell you a story..."

And suddenly, silence.

You could hear a pin drop. Because stories *still matter*. Not only to children, but also to adults.

So, this is the story *before* the story.

The story of the *planter*.

The one who never knew what his obedience and faith would grow into.

Craig Minty – 2025

P.S. *Oh—and just so you know... I'm 181cm now.*
Sorry, Zacchaeus. Looks like I did grow up after all.
But you got to meet Him—so you win.

Chapter One:
The Seed in the Dust

The young boy's fingers pressed into the dry, crumbly earth, curling protectively around the tiny seed as though shielding it from the fierce and unforgiving gaze of the sun. The soil was coarse, stubbornly resisting before giving way to the tender insistence of the boy's small hands. Dust clung to the creases of his knuckles, forming pale lines across skin already browned by long days spent playing beneath the open sky. The heat rising from the ground licked at his skin like the breath of a kiln, wrapping around him in waves that pulsed with the rhythm of the land itself.

Above him, the midday sun blazed mercilessly, suspended like a golden coin in a bleached, cloudless sky. It was a scorching summer day—the kind of day when even the stones seemed to sweat—and certainly not the most sensible choice for planting. But something about this day, this hour, had been chosen. And Abner had not questioned it. Today was not a day for playing... today, he had a purpose.

In the near distance, the city of Jericho shimmered like a mirage. Its whitewashed buildings wavered behind curtains of heat, their edges softened by the illusion of movement—like dreams waiting to be caught, or stories waiting to be told. The city pulsed quietly beneath the sun, its silence broken only by the bleating of distant goats and the occasional shout of a trader or shepherd echoing across the valley.

Along the roadside where he knelt, rows of olive trees stood like ancient sentinels. Their gnarled limbs twisted skyward, grey-green leaves fluttering with a sound like whispered prayers. These trees had watched countless seasons pass. They had borne witness to the footsteps of travellers, merchants, soldiers, priests, and pilgrims—some walking with purpose, others simply with weariness. In their crooked branches, sparrows nested, their tiny bodies rustling the leaves as they darted in and out seemingly playfully. The trees offered more than fruit; they provided shade for the desperate, oil for the anointed, and a sense of familiarity to the landscape. These trees stood as both memory and promise.

Abner hesitated, wondering.

His fingers hovered just above the small hole he and his father had dug earlier that morning, the soil still warm to the touch. He could feel his heartbeat in his fingertips, each pulse steady and loud, as though his very breath was connected to the seed he held.

This was no ordinary planting.

He was only nine, and yet something in him knew—deep and wordless—that this moment mattered. It wasn't just farming. It wasn't just a lesson or a task. It was a kind of liturgy, a sacred gesture. To him, the seed was more than a seed. It was a hope, a trust, a prayer pressed into the earth.

A beginning.

He felt the weight of his father's gaze behind him—not heavy, but present. Expectant, yet never forceful. There was kindness in it. A silent encouragement that wrapped around him like shade on a hot day. Abner didn't turn around. He didn't need to. He could feel Eliab there, steady as the earth beneath them. Watching. Waiting. Trusting.

With a slow breath and a strange calmness in his chest, Abner lowered his hand. He moved with a kind of care and precision he didn't know he possessed, as though the seed were something sacred. As though it might break if handled too quickly. He placed it gently into the hollow they had dug together, cradling it for a moment longer before letting it rest in the soil's embrace. It was barely larger than the tip of his smallest finger—dark, dry, unimpressive. Ordinary.

Yet to Abner, it was something far more.

He stared at the seed for a moment, half expecting it to stir, to shine, to suddenly spring to life. But it remained still. Quiet. Hidden. He smiled anyway. Leaning closer, he closed his eyes and whispered, almost shyly, "Grow, little tree."

His voice was soft, almost lost in the breeze, but he meant every word.

Then, with careful hands, he gathered the loose mound of soil they had set aside and covered the seed, letting it fall like a blanket over something sleeping. Abner repeated this and then patted the earth down gently with his open palm—once, then again—until the surface was smooth.

It was a single, simple act.

But it mattered.

It mattered in the way a first step matters. In the way a promise whispered into darkness can still echo for years after.

Eliab crouched beside him, one knee cracking as he lowered himself down with the slow ease of a man accustomed to work. His beard, thick and streaked with grey, glistened with the sweat of the day. He looked at the small patch of dirt with a nod of approval, his eyes not on the ground, but on the boy.

"Good," he said, voice low and warm. "One day, this will be a mighty tree."

Abner looked up, squinting through the sunlight that poured over his father's shoulder. "But it's so small, Abba," he said, puzzled. "It doesn't even look alive."

Eliab chuckled softly and reached for the cloth tucked into his belt, swiping it across his brow before draping it around his neck. "All things start small, my son. Even the greatest of trees. Even us."

Abner tilted his head. His brow furrowed in thought. The words stirred something in him, but he couldn't quite grasp them. "What do you mean?"

Eliab sat back on his heels, stretching his arms behind him until his shoulders gave a soft, familiar crack. Then, with the slow precision of a man who knew the land and respected it, he placed both hands into the soil around the seed's resting place and pressed the earth gently, firming it with care, Abner's eyes observing closely his father's teaching of planting.

"Sycamores are strong," he said, his voice low, like a lore being passed down. "They take root even in hard, stubborn ground. Not every tree can do that. But sycamores... they dig deep. They search for water with a quiet determination, winding their roots down until they find what they need. And when their roots are deep—when they've truly settled into the earth—they begin to grow wide, to stretch outward and hold firm. Even when the storms come, they don't topple easily."

He paused, his fingers brushing away a stray pebble from the top of the soil. Then he turned to his son, and the glint in his eyes was not just from the sun.

"One day," he said softly, "travellers will rest beneath its shade—the tired, the old, maybe even the broken-hearted. Children will climb its limbs, scrape their knees, and laugh from its highest branches. Maybe you will, Abner, or maybe even your children." Eliab said with a slight chuckle.

Abner's face twisted slightly with concern. He looked at the patch of earth, now calm and undisturbed, as if unsure it had really received anything at all. "But... what if it doesn't grow?" he asked, his voice caught somewhere between worry and wonder.

Eliab didn't flinch. He didn't scold. His response came without hesitation, like the answer had been stored in him for years, ready for this very moment.

"Then we plant again," he said, with a quiet strength that made the words feel larger than they were. "But I believe this seed will grow. I believe it's meant to." He looked at the spot again, then back toward his son. "Who knows what purpose the Lord has for this one? We don't need to know everything. God Himself does. And He always has a purpose—even for the smallest things. Especially for the smallest things."

He reached out and ruffled Abner's hair, the gesture full of affection and anchored in something deeper than just love. It was a father's blessing in motion.

Just then, the breeze shifted.

It was the kind of shift that made the hairs on your arms lift slightly, not from cold but from awareness. The air changed. The sounds of the road grew faint, and the leaves of the nearby olive trees stirred gently. The breeze carried with it the mingled scent of dry dust, crushed olive leaves, and the distant sweetness of figs ripening in hidden groves beyond Jericho's edge. It was as if the land itself had taken a breath and exhaled peace. And yet, the breath that stirred the trees was no ordinary breeze—it moved with intention, as if carrying something unseen.

Abner sat cross-legged beside his father, the red dirt warm beneath his legs. He gazed at the small mound of soil in front of him, eyes locked on something unseen. In his mind, he pictured roots already stirring—slow, delicate tendrils stretching out in the darkness, seeking water, seeking life. He imagined them unfurling like arms waking from sleep, yawning beneath the surface in search of the deep.

The idea fascinated him.

The idea that something so tiny, so easily overlooked, so completely buried—could grow into something strong enough to hold birds and boys alike... it stirred something inside him that felt bigger than understanding.

He wanted to believe it.

He wanted to see it.

He wanted it to happen right now.

"Will it grow quickly?" he asked at last, his voice quieter now, almost hoping for a miracle in the answer.

Eliab smiled again and tousled his hair with a gentle hand. "Not quickly," he said with a slow shake of his head. "But it will grow. Slowly... but surely. And you'll see it, Abner. Just be patient."

He paused, then looked at him more intently, his tone soft but deliberate.

"Patient," he repeated with slightly more emphasis as he looked directly at his son.

Abner sighed, his breath stirring a small puff of dust at his feet. It rose like smoke and quickly disappeared into the shimmering heat, leaving only the faintest trace behind. His shoulders slumped. There was no rebellion in his posture, just the quiet disappointment of a boy caught between imagination and reality.

Patience felt like punishment.

He wanted branches now. He wanted shade today. He had imagined planting the seed in the morning and swinging from its limbs by nightfall. The thought of waiting—not just days or weeks, but years—was almost unbearable. What was the point of planting something he couldn't enjoy now?

He kicked at the ground with the side of his foot, sending a small clump of dry dirt tumbling. "I don't want to wait," he muttered, frustration riding the edge of his voice.

Eliab smiled—not mockingly, not dismissively, but with the kind of smile only a father can give. A knowing one. A remembering one. A loving one. He pushed himself to his feet with a low groan, the weight of age and labour stiff in his joints. Brushing the dust from his tunic, he looked down at his son, and the heat of the day seemed to soften around them.

"I know," he said gently. "I understand, Abner. Neither do I, my son."

He reached out his hand.

Abner hesitated for only a moment before slipping his fingers into his father's palm. His hand was small, almost swallowed by the rough, calloused strength of Eliab's. There was safety in that grip—an anchor in the unknown.

Eliab pulled him up, lifting him into the light with effortless ease. Once standing, he didn't let go.

"But waiting," Eliab continued, his eyes scanning the horizon for a moment, "is part of life. It's part of what is called… becoming."

He let the word hang in the air, as though it deserved space to settle.

"Becoming is where…" He paused again, searching not for the

Planted for a purpose

right words, but for the truest ones. "It's where we grow into the thing we were always meant to be. Not something forced or hurried. It's not where we start, Abner—but it's what's already within us. And it's through time, through joy and sorrow, success and failure, through moments just like this... that we become."

Abner looked up, blinking against the sunlight that rimmed his father's beard like firelight. Something in those words landed deep, even if he didn't fully understand them. Not yet.

Still holding his father's hand, he smiled.

Not a wide grin, but the kind of smile that lingers in the corners—small, quiet, sincere.

He wondered, not for the first time, whether every Hebrew boy had a father like his. A father who spoke wisdom without sounding proud. One who worked with his hands but taught with his heart. One who seemed to understand the world in a way that made it feel less frightening.

Abner didn't say it aloud.

But he was so grateful for his abba.

"Come, son, your mother will be expecting us," Eliab said, nodding toward the path.

They began walking together, the dust soft beneath their sandals, rising faintly with each step.

Their home came into view a few minutes later—a simple dwelling, unassuming and modest, like most others scattered along the outskirts of Jericho. The house looked as though it had grown out of the very land it rested upon, shaped from sunbaked clay and local stone, its walls the colour of the surrounding hills. Flat-roofed and square in shape, the structure bore the humble character of hard-working hands. Its small windows were little more than narrow slits, designed to keep out the heat more than let in the light.

The outer walls bore faint lines from where the mudbrick had dried unevenly in the sun, and a low courtyard wall, half-tumbled in places, marked the edge of their home's domain. A fig tree stood in one corner, its leaves offering a patch of trembling shade across the worn threshold. A large clay jar, used for water or washing, sat beside the doorway, its rounded surface stained from years of use.

There was no grandeur to the place, no sign of wealth or luxury. But there was a quiet warmth in its worn timbers and weathered stone—a sense that this house had known laughter and tears, had held stories within its walls, and had been shaped not just by hands, but by love.

To Abner, it was the most familiar place in the world.

But just as they reached the low wall that marked the edge of their home, Abner stopped.

He turned; his eyes pulled once more to the small mound of earth they had left behind. A thought stirred within him—small, but urgent.

"Here," Eliab said, stepping toward the large clay jar beside the doorway, its surface cool and slightly cracked from years of use. Abner reached up as his father gently tipped the jar, and together they guided the stream of water into the small clay cup resting on the rim. The cup felt rough against Abner's fingertips—the way handmade things often do—and he cradled it in both hands with care.

"Pour this where you planted the seed," Eliab said quietly, without waiting for a reply. It wasn't a command. It was instinct.

He walked quickly, the water sloshing gently as he moved. The sun caught the rippling surface and scattered tiny flecks of light across his tunic.

Reaching the place where the seed now lay hidden, Abner knelt again. He poured the water from the clay cup slowly, reverently, letting it trickle through his fingers and into the soil. He didn't want the water to drench the area but to soak through the disturbed soil gently. The dry earth darkened immediately where the drops landed, soaking in the gift like something thirsty finally being satisfied. A quiet sigh seemed to rise from the ground itself, or perhaps from Abner's chest.

He watched the water disappear, and for a moment, time stilled.

Footsteps approached softly behind him.

"Why do we water it?" Abner asked as he stood, tilting the empty cup slightly to let the last drops fall. His voice was calm now, curious, not restless.

Eliab didn't answer right away.

Instead, he looked down the road that wound back toward the trees, toward the city, toward whatever future might come.

"Because faith," he said at last, "must be tended."

Abner frowned slightly and glanced up at him. "What do you mean?"

Eliab met his son's gaze with a steady warmth. "God told Adam to tend the garden," he said. "To watch over it. Protect it. Nourish it. That command hasn't changed. Whether it's a seed in the ground or something deep inside your heart... if it's meant to grow, you must care for it. You can't just bury it and forget. That is the task God gave Adam, and it's now up to us to continue."

Abner nodded slowly, even as the meaning fluttered just beyond complete understanding. But something in those words settled within him, not in his mind, but somewhere deeper, beneath his ribs, where things are felt rather than thought. Like a second seed, gently planted by a father's wisdom and watered by wonder.

He didn't know yet how much that moment would matter.

But one day, he would.

As they began the walk back toward their home, past the grove of olive trees whispering in the breeze, past the goats napping in the shade of the courtyard wall, past the uneven stone boundary that marked their neighbour's field, Abner moved a little slower than before.

The day was still hot, and the sun still high, but something in him had quietened.

He glanced over his shoulder.

There was nothing remarkable to see—just a patch of damp earth beneath an open sky—no sign of what had been buried there. No marker. No name. Just soil, darkened slightly from water, soon to dry and look like every other patch of land around it.

No one walking past would give it a second glance. No one would believe it held any worth.

But his father had said it would grow.

And his father had never been wrong before—not about important things. To Abner, this was important.

So, Abner made a decision. A quiet one. A boy's decision, yet no less sacred for its simplicity.

He would believe, too.

Not because he could see branches or leaves yet.

Not because the soil had stirred.

Not because there was any evidence that the tree existed at all.

But because someone he trusted—someone who had walked beside him, dug the hole with him, stood in the same sun and spoken with gentle strength—believed it was already there.

And that, for now, was enough.

Chapter Two:
Seeds and Grains

The scent of warm bread greeted Abner the moment he stepped into the cool dimness of their stone house. It wrapped around him like a blanket, thick with the fragrance of flour, yeast, and hearth smoke. He drew in a deep breath without thinking, the kind of breath one only takes when returning to something deeply familiar.

His feet, still dusty from the path outside, padded softly across the worn threshold. The earth clung to him, but the moment he crossed into the shade of home, the dust seemed to belong there too.

Inside, the light was gentler, muted and golden. It sifted through the narrow windows and the linen hangings draped across the inner walls, casting soft shadows that danced slightly in the breeze. The thick stone walls held back the heat of the midday sun, and the air carried the hum of stillness, the kind only found in places that are lived in with love.

It wasn't a grand house.

But it breathed with life.

The atmosphere within was alive with quiet movement—sunlight catching in the folds of fabric, the faint crackle from the coals in the hearth, the rhythm of daily work. But beneath it all was something deeper: memory. Care. The kind of love that doesn't announce itself, but settles into the corners of a home and never leaves.

His mother, Naamah, knelt beside the grinding stone in the central room—the heart of the house. Her back was strong and straight, her posture shaped by years of labour and grace. Her arms moved with practised ease, rolling the heavy upper stone back and forth across a handful of golden wheat. The sound it made was steady and grounding—a soft rasping rhythm like the turning of time itself. The grain surrendered slowly, bit by bit, transformed into flour beneath her hands.

It filled the room like a gentle drumbeat.

Ancient. Necessary. Sacred.

Abner paused near the doorway and stood there, still holding the clay cup, though the last drop of water had long since soaked into the earth. He listened not just with his ears, but with memory.

That sound.

It was one of the first he had ever known.

Long before he understood words, before he could walk, before he had even formed a single memory, that sound had been there. The sound of grain being ground by steady hands. The sound of nourishment being prepared. The sound of his mother shaping life from the harvest.

The sound of care.

The sound of home.

The sound of his mother's hands.

Naamah glanced up at him, her dark eyes bright with recognition and the soft, familiar smile of adoration that always found its way to her lips when she looked at her son.

"Ah, you're back," she said warmly, brushing her palms together. A cloud of flour puffed into the air, and a pale smudge streaked her cheek, though she didn't seem to notice—or care. It was part of the work, part of her.

"Did you and your father finish already?"

Abner nodded and smiled. He didn't speak—he didn't need to. The rhythm of the house invited quiet.

He lowered himself beside her, folding his legs beneath him on the cool stone floor. As he settled, the room seemed to sigh around him, releasing a breath it hadn't realised it was holding. This was the heart of their home—the place where hands worked, where stories were shared, and where silence felt safe.

Naamah returned to her task, the rhythmic grinding resuming beneath her steady hands. The circular motion of the upper stone was seamless, almost graceful, as she leaned forward and back, her muscles moving with quiet strength and memory.

Abner watched in silence, his eyes following the familiar motion. There was something intensely captivating about it. Not just the motion itself, but the meaning within it. This wasn't just routine. This wasn't just work. It was something closer to worship.

The bread that would come from this flour wasn't simply nourishment. It was legacy. It was love given shape and heat.

"Ima," he said softly, his voice barely more than a breath, "I remember when Savta used to do this with you."

Naamah's hands stilled.

For a moment, she didn't look at him. She placed the stone aside with care, her hands resting lightly on her knees as she exhaled, slowly, as though releasing a memory she'd been holding in.

Then she looked at him, and her smile returned, gentler now. Full of something deeper than the present.

"Yes," she said, her voice low and warm. "She loved to work beside me. She always said the sound of grinding wheat was the sound of a house preparing for life."

She paused, the corners of her mouth lifting just a little more.

"And after you were born, she would always add—'and food for my favourite grandson.'"

Abner lowered his gaze, a shy smile playing at his lips. He reached out and traced a slow finger through the fine dusting of flour that had settled on the floor, drawing invisible shapes into the powder.

"I used to hear it when I was a baby, didn't I?"

"You did," she said, her voice softening into memory. "You would lie in the basket by the door, swaddled tight like a little loaf waiting to rise."

She smiled, eyes shining not just with the present moment but with the glow of days long past.

"Your eyes would flutter open at the sound of the grinding stone, then slowly close again. But every time we stopped, you'd stir—little arms flailing, little cries escaping. And your Savta would laugh and shake her head and say, 'Ah, he knows the work must go on.'"

Abner smiled too. The image wrapped around him like a warm blanket.

He could almost hear her voice—soft and lilting, warm like the breeze before dawn. He could almost smell the hint of rose oil she used to dab behind her ears. He could almost see her hands, strong and lined with age, folding dough with the quiet force of a woman who had lived through joy and sorrow and kept going.

"But now..." he paused. The words came before he had time to guard them. "It's just you."

The silence that followed was not heavy, not cold. It was packed—full of memory, full of love, and full of something unspoken that hung between them like incense.

Naamah leaned toward him and brushed her fingers gently

through his curls. A few strands caught the flour still on her fingertips, leaving pale trails in his dark hair. Her touch was slow and reverent, like the closing of a scroll.

"Yes," she said softly. "For now, it is just me."

She didn't say more right away. She let the silence breathe, and in that space, something sacred lingered.

Then she added, her voice low and sure, "But you are here now, Abner. And one day, you will teach your own children, just as she taught me."

Abner blinked, uncertain.

He didn't feel old enough to teach anyone anything. Not yet. Not even close.

But the idea that what they did—the planting, the grinding, the kneading—might live on through him, passed down like a song or a blessing... it stirred something in his chest. Something bigger than he could name.

Something like a seed.

A giggle broke the stillness—high-pitched, bubbling with innocence, and entirely out of place in the hushed reverence of flour and memory.

Abner turned toward the corner of the room, a familiar smile already forming. There, sitting cross-legged on a woven mat beside the loom, was his younger sister, Hila. Her curls bounced as she rocked back and forth in glee, and in her small, chubby hands, she clutched a scrap of blue cloth, waving it triumphantly above her head like a battle banner.

"Hila," Abner grinned. "Are you weaving... or starting a war?"

She squealed with laughter and tossed the cloth into the air. It fluttered like a bird before landing in a crumpled heap beside her. She clapped her hands in delight, utterly unbothered by its fall.

Naamah glanced over her shoulder and chuckled, her eyes crinkling with affection. "One day, perhaps she'll sit here and help me," she said, turning back to the grinding stone, "just as Savta helped me."

"Maybe," Abner said with a smirk. "If she ever stops chewing on your weaving."

Naamah laughed—a sound full of brightness, like sunlight caught in stone. It was a sound that had soaked into the very walls of the house, a song the timbers surely knew by heart.

"Yes, one day," she agreed. "But for now, she is content to pull every loose thread she can find."

She leaned in closer to Abner, her voice lowering into that special tone mothers use when teasing with love. "And for now," she added, brushing her flour-covered hands through his dark curls, "I still have you."

The white powder clung to his hair, settling like snow on a mountain goat. For a moment, Abner looked like some ancient little sage, conjured from the dust and bread of the earth.

He rolled his eyes in mock protest, but the tug of a smile betrayed him.

"I suppose," he muttered, though the grin that crept across his face said otherwise.

Abner leaned forward and pressed his small hands into the flour-dusted dough resting in the wide clay bowl. It gave way beneath his fingers, warm and springy—alive with the slow magic of yeast, heat, and time. He spread his fingers, letting the dough push back as he kneaded, mimicking the movements he had watched his mother do countless times.

The dough clung to his fingertips like a playful friend, and for a moment, he felt almost grown.

From the corner of the room, Hila clapped her hands again, her delight bubbling into the air like water on a fire. She watched her older brother with wide-eyed joy, laughing at the sight of him plunging his hands into the mixture.

Abner made a silly face—eyes crossed, lips puckered like a dried fig—and Hila shrieked with laughter. Her giggles sent her tumbling backwards onto her mat, limbs flailing in the air like a startled beetle. She paused for a second, stunned by the fall, then burst into even louder laughter, rolling from side to side, completely undone by joy.

And then the door creaked open.

The soft light of late afternoon beamed into the house, golden and low. It stretched across the floor like a welcome, touching the edges of their world with warmth. The scent of sunlit earth entered with it.

Eliab stepped inside, the corners of his robe streaked with dust and sun-stained from the day's labour. He paused just inside the threshold. His presence shifted the room's stillness, like a breeze entering after a long stillness, quiet, but unmistakably felt.

Naamah looked up from her place near the hearth, brushing her hands on her apron. "You're back just in time," she said with a smile that lingered behind her eyes.

Abner straightened, eyes gleaming. "Abba! What's that?" he asked, pointing to the cloth bundle his father held in both hands.

Eliab smiled as he approached, the lines in his face deepened by sunlight and contentment. "A treat for Shabbat," he said, setting the bundle gently on the low table.

He unwrapped it slowly, as though it held something precious. Inside were a small handful of fresh dates—glossy and dark—and a tiny jar of honey, sealed with wax and tied with a thin strand of reed.

Abner leaned forward, his hands still dusted in flour, fingers stretching toward the treasure. But before he could reach it, Naamah's hand came down with gentle precision, swatting his wrist with a mother's grace.

"Not yet," she said, her voice firm but filled with affection. "Finish the dough first."

Abner pulled back, grinning sheepishly as he returned to the bowl.

"Just like his father," Eliab said with a chuckle as he lowered himself beside them, his knees cracking softly as he sat. "The boy is the same way I was—always in a hurry."

He reached over and tousled Abner's hair, sending a puff of flour into the air.

"But good things take time, my son. Like my abba—your sabba—used to tell me: 'Rushed bread burns. Rushed plans break.'"

Eliab tousled Abner's flour-dusted curls again, then paused, his hand lingering for a moment before settling at his side. He studied his son's face more closely—the curve of his brow, the quiet thought behind his eyes.

"Do you remember how you planted the seed today?" he asked, his voice calm and measured.

Abner nodded, glancing briefly toward the door as though he could see it again. "Yes, Abba."

He hesitated.

"You said it would grow into a mighty tree."

Eliab's expression softened, the lines of his face shifting with tenderness. "It will," he said assuredly. "But not tomorrow. And not next week."

He turned his gaze toward the dough resting between Abner's small hands.

"It will take time, just like this bread. If we rush it—if we don't give it room to rise—it will come out hard... bitter. Difficult to chew. Difficult to share."

He met Abner's eyes again. "A tree is no different. Life is no different."

Naamah, still at the hearth, smiled without looking up. "I told him the same thing," she said gently. "Waiting is part of growing."

Eliab nodded slowly. His voice dropped, growing quieter but deeper, like a stream flowing beneath the surface.

"And tending," he added. "Waiting alone is not enough. What we plant must be protected."

He reached for the cup of water nearby and held it up, letting a few drops fall back into the bowl. "If a young shoot rises and no one guards it, the animals may trample it. The weeds may choke it. The sun may burn it."

Abner looked down at his hands, still buried in the soft, living dough. It was changing under his touch even now. Becoming.

"So, I have to protect it?" he asked, the weight of the question heavier than his voice suggested.

Eliab nodded.

"Yes," he said. "As we must protect the things that matter most."

He placed a hand on Abner's shoulder, firm but full of affection, as though anchoring him in place.

"Like family," he continued. His gaze flicked to Hila, who had resumed waving her scrap of cloth like a triumphant queen. His smile grew.

"You are the firstborn, Abner. That means something. It is not about being better or stronger. It's about responsibility."

He looked back at his son, his tone now a blend of love and legacy.

"Because of the birthright, it is your role to take care of this family. To protect. To remember. To grow strong—not just for yourself, but for those who will one day need your strength."

Abner didn't speak.

But he heard it.

Every word rooted itself deeper than the last.

The golden light of late afternoon filtered through the narrow window, casting long streaks of warmth across the stone walls. It danced across the uneven surface, flickering like firelight against the textured clay, and bathed the floor in soft, amber hues. The warmth pooled around their feet, turning the clay beneath them into something that felt almost alive.

Naamah stood slowly, placing a steadying hand on her back as she straightened. The quiet strength of her posture never wavered.

"Come now," she said gently. "We must finish before the sun sets."

Eliab shifted, rising to his feet in one practised motion. He reached over and scooped Hila into his arms. She squealed in delight, her legs kicking with wild abandon, and her laughter rang through the room like wind chimes caught in a playful breeze.

He kissed the top of her head, her curls brushing his cheek like feathers. "And you, little one," he murmured, rocking her slightly, "you will grow too."

Hila beamed up at him, the joy of the moment radiating from her face. Her small fingers reached up to tug curiously at his beard, fascinated by its coarseness. She giggled again, content in the safety of her father's arms.

Abner returned to the dough, his hands sinking once more into its yielding warmth. He pressed gently, feeling the way it resisted and gave way, the way it held the memory of his fingers.

Around him, the house glowed with the scent of flour and honey, the rich tang of wood smoke, and the low hush of the evening drawing near. The rhythm of his father's voice lingered in the air, not loud, but lasting, settled into the corners of the room like a quiet blessing.

He didn't know if the tree would grow quickly.

He didn't know if he'd still be here when it was tall enough to climb.

But as the last light of day slipped across the floor like a whispered promise, touching the dough, the stones, and the folds of his mother's apron in a final golden caress, one thought took root within him.

The tree was growing.

Even if he couldn't see it yet.

Chapter Three:
The Most Special Shabbat

As the golden light of the setting sun stretched long fingers across the stone walls of their home, the rhythm of the house began to change. The sounds grew quieter, slower. The laughter faded into smiles. The work gave way to something gentler.

Naamah moved through the room with quiet purpose, her steps deliberate, her body attuned to a rhythm older than words. The clay walls, kissed now by amber light, seemed to exhale with her. The day was ending. And something sacred was about to begin.

One by one, she lit the small oil lamps nestled along the carved wooden shelf—simple clay vessels, blackened by years of faithful use. Her hands, dusted faintly with flour and olive oil, moved with grace and familiarity. Each wick drank from its oil and rose into flame, casting a soft glow that grew with every lamp she touched. The light flickered across her cheeks, gilding her features with a quiet radiance. In her eyes, the flames were mirrored—tiny stars shimmering in pools of memory.

She whispered the ancient blessing, her voice reverent and steady, not loud, but enough to fill the room.

"Baruch atah Adonai, Eloheinu Melech ha'olam,
asher kid'shanu b'mitzvotav,
v'tzivanu l'hadlik ner shel Shabbat…"

| *Planted for a purpose*

Blessed are You, O Lord our God, King of the Universe, who has sanctified us with His commandments and commanded us to light the Shabbat lights.

The words did not simply hang in the air. They settled into it, like soft rain into dry soil. They soaked into the clay walls, into the folds of garments, into the beating hearts of those who listened. Generations had spoken this blessing before her, and she felt them now—those who had lit lamps in Egypt, in the wilderness, in Canaan, in exile, and now here, outside Jericho.

The glow filled the room, not with brightness, but with warmth, like a soft blanket pulled across a weary soul. It softened every edge: the harsh lines of the stone walls, the shadows crouched in corners, the wornness in their eyes. All were wrapped now in light.

The small house, so modest in its construction, became holy in that moment, not because of its bricks or its bowls or its beams, but because of the presence that settled in with the light.

Shadows retreated, as though in deference. The amber haze gently pushed them away, replacing them with an almost tangible calmness. Outside, the sun sank lower, brushing the tops of olive trees with gold. Inside, the aroma of freshly baked bread mingled with the sweetness of olive oil and the sharp tang of herbs crushed by hand. It filled every breath. The very air was thick with comfort.

This was more than the end of a day.

This was the ushering in of Shabbat—the queen of the week, entering not with trumpets or parade, but with light... and rest... and peace.

And in the heart of it all stood Naamah. A woman of strength, hands worn by work and softened by love. A mother. A daughter. A keeper of tradition. Her eyes reflected not just fire, but hope.

And for a moment, the whole world seemed to pause—just long enough to notice that something eternal was happening.

Abner sat beside his father, their shoulders touching, the space between them filled with a comforting stillness. He leaned slightly against Eliab's side, the rough weave of his father's tunic brushing against his cheek like the fabric of memory. The solid weight of Eliab's arm pressed gently into his own, a quiet but unwavering presence. It was more than physical warmth—it was safety. It was belonging.

No stone wall, no roof overhead, no door bolted shut could offer what this closeness did.

Here, in this simple home bathed in candlelight and Shabbat stillness, there was love. There was happiness. And there was safety. The kind of safety that wrapped around your soul and told it not to be afraid.

Eliab reached forward, his hand steady as he took hold of the Kiddush cup. It was a simple vessel, made of clay, worn smooth by years of use. The rim was slightly chipped, and its glaze had dulled over time, but to Abner, it seemed more precious than gold.

His father held it with quiet reverence, lifting it slowly until it caught the light of the oil lamps. The flickering flames reflected on its surface, like tongues of fire dancing in silent worship.

And then Eliab began to speak.

His voice was strong and full, shaped by faith and years of repetition—not rote, but rhythm. Familiar. Firm. Like the heartbeat of their people.

"Baruch atah Adonai, Eloheinu Melech ha'olam, borei p'ri hagafen..."

Blessed are You, O Lord our God, King of the Universe, who brings forth the fruit of the vine.

| *Planted for a purpose*

The words were ancient. Abner had heard them every Friday evening of his life. They were as predictable as the setting sun, as familiar as the scent of bread in the oven. And yet... tonight, something felt different.

Maybe it was the way the candlelight shimmered on the rim of the cup, casting soft glows against the walls like halos made of flame.

Maybe it was the sound of his father's voice—weightier than usual, as if every word had been carried up from someplace deep within. Or maybe it was something inside Abner himself.

Something stirring.

Something alive.

Something reaching upward, like a sprout pushing through soil in search of sunlight, breaking into a world it couldn't yet see.

Eliab finished the blessing and passed the cup to Naamah. Her hands cradled it with quiet grace. She brought it to her lips, sipping with the careful respect of one tasting tradition, then handed it gently to Abner.

He took it in both hands, holding it as if it might slip through his fingers—not from weight, but from meaning. The clay felt cool against his skin, ancient and sacred. He could almost feel the past in its shape—his father's hands, his grandfather's, maybe even his great-grandfather's. He had never asked, and he wouldn't now.

He brought it to his lips and took the tiniest sip.

The wine was sweet—sweeter and richer than he expected it to taste. It clung to his tongue like a song that refused to end. It lingered there, not just in taste but in sensation, as if it carried a message meant not for his mouth but for his spirit.

It tasted of fruit... but also of promise.

Of covenant.

Of promise.

Of something yet to be.

The blessings continued.

Eliab reached for the braided challah bread, golden and still warm from the hearth. Its surface shimmered slightly with a glaze of honey and oil, and the soft weave of the dough spoke of patience, care, and ancient rhythms passed down through hands like his. He held it in both palms, lifting it with the same reverence he had shown the wine.

He pressed a gentle kiss to its crown, a gesture as old as their people—an act of gratitude for God's provision.

Then, with steady hands, he broke it in two.

A soft crack echoed in the room, followed by the faint whisper of crumbs scattering across the table like seeds sown into waiting soil.

Eliab passed the first piece to Naamah. She received it with a quiet nod, her eyes shining in the lamplight. Then to Abner, who took his portion with both hands, feeling the warmth of the bread seeping into his palms. And finally, to Hila.

She squealed with delight and reached out with both hands, clutching the piece like treasure. Her curls bounced as she wriggled in place, her eyes wide with anticipation. She bit gently into the soft edge and grinned, cheeks full and glowing.

Abner couldn't take his eyes off her.

There was something about the way she moved—uninhibited, joyful, alive. She didn't know she was lighting up the room, just by being. She didn't realise that her laughter softened shadows and stitched warmth into the air.

She was simply and beautifully, Hila.

And that was enough.

Abner smiled, his chest swelling with something he hadn't quite felt before. His heart felt so full—so rich and overflowing—his heart almost ached.

She brought joy.

Not through words or deeds. Not through effort.

She brought joy without trying.

She brought joy through her simple presence.

The meal that followed was humble, as it was every Shabbat—there was no silver, no feast of royal splendour, no fine wines or exotic spices from far-off lands.

And yet... tonight, it tasted richer than a king's table.

The *challah* remained warm, its crust golden and crisp, giving way to soft, pillowy insides that still held the heat of the hearth. Roasted vegetables—carrots, onions, and thick slices of aubergine—glistened with olive oil, their edges just beginning to char, releasing the sweetness from within. A bowl of lentils, fragrant with garlic, cumin, and salt, sat at the centre of the table. Its scent alone was enough to stir memories of comfort, of full bellies and quiet evenings.

Beside them lay a modest dish of olives from the market—black and green, wrinkled and gleaming, brined to perfection—and a small bundle of dates wrapped in cloth, gathered from the orchard near the western edge of town. Naamah, smiling with a glint of mischief, had even added a few figs she'd saved for a special night. They were soft to the touch, their insides bursting with sweetness, like sunbursts soaked in honey.

Abner took slow bites, letting each flavour linger on his tongue longer than he usually allowed. He wasn't one to savour food—meals were often a blur between hunger and satisfaction—but tonight was different.

Tonight, he was aware.

Every bite carried a weight.

Every flavour seemed to unfold in layers: the warmth of cumin, the burst of sweetness from the figs, the crisp edge of the bread, the briny sharpness of the olives. It was as if something in him had changed. As if the act of burying that small seed in the ground earlier that day had awakened a new way of seeing... and tasting... and being.

Maybe it was the way the air now felt thicker, not heavy with heat, but hushed—as if the house itself was holding its breath, listening.

Maybe it was the light—warmer, slower, wrapping everything in gold and silence.

Maybe it was because, in the planting of that tiny seed, something in him had taken root as well.

As they ate, Eliab spoke, as he always did on Shabbat, but Abner noticed the rhythm of his father's voice more than usual. It was deep and calm, like a river that never ran dry—never rushed, never loud, but always moving.

"Six days we labour," Eliab said, his voice carrying over the clink of dishes and the rustle of fabric, "but on the seventh, we rest."

He paused, letting the words rest too.

"Just as the Lord rested after He created the heavens and the earth. And as Moses wrote in the Law: *Remember the Shabbat, and keep it holy.*"

Abner chewed slowly, the food no longer just nourishing his body—it was stirring something deeper. He stared at the small lamp in the centre of the table, its flame swaying slightly with the breath of the room and wondered if rest was more than stillness. If rest was more than stopping.

His father had spoken earlier of patience—of waiting for trees to grow, of time and tending.

But now...

Now another layer was being folded into that wisdom, like oil into flour.

Rest.

Not just to wait, but to trust. To believe that even when nothing seems to be happening, something is. Something is growing.

Even in the dark.

Even when it is unseen.

There was a time to labour and a time to rest. These were the rhythms of creation, the cycles etched into the bones of the world from the very beginning. Abner had heard the words before, repeated like a melody at every Shabbat, but tonight they settled in him differently. They planted themselves like seeds of their own.

He wondered—his young mind stretching like a vine, slow and searching, reaching toward a light he couldn't yet name. *Did the seed outside know it was time to rest?*

Was it aware, in whatever way a seed could be, that now was not the moment to rise but to wait? To sleep in the dark, not with fear, but with trust? To be still, even buried, nourished by a hope that had not yet taken shape?

Perhaps I should have told it, he thought suddenly, *before I covered it with soil and gave it water.*

He frowned, not in worry, but in deep thought. *How would it know what to do?*

The idea seemed impossibly large—yet somehow, true. Life, it seemed, did not need to be told. It knew. It waited. It rose when the time was right. Perhaps even when God told it to. The idea grew even larger than Abner expected with that final thought.

Across the room, Naamah moved with quiet intention. She poured warm water into a small clay basin, steam rising like breath into the lamplight, and set it near Hila. The little one waddled over, eyes bright with mischief and delight. She plunged her chubby hands into the basin without hesitation, squealing at the warmth and splashing far more than she washed.

Water dripped across the stone floor in bright little trails, but no one corrected her.

Her joy—wild, unrestrained and unmeasured—was part of the holiness, too.

Abner watched her for a long moment. He had seen her do this dozens of times before, but now... something shifted in his gaze.

"She is growing," he thought, the realisation rising quietly within him.

He no longer saw her merely as the baby of the family—no longer just a source of giggles or messes or half-chewed figs.

She was becoming.

Someone who, one day, would stretch into her own shape, rise into her own story.

The thought stirred something deep in his emotions. He looked around the room, as if seeing it all anew.

Everything around him was growing.

The fields outside, heavy with ripening wheat, bowing slightly under the weight of promise. The vines beyond the walls, coiling upward, bearing fruit he had not planted.

The olive trees along the road, old and gnarled, yet constantly pushing out new leaves.

His sister.

His understanding.

Even the silence itself felt richer now, fuller, like soil after rain.

And somewhere outside—beyond the walls of their home, beneath

| *Planted for a purpose*

the surface of the earth, where light did not yet reach—the seed.

Small. Hidden. Silent.

But not forgotten.

It was waiting.

And in its waiting... it was becoming.

After the meal, they remained seated around the low table, their bodies full and their hearts hushed. The oil lamps now stood as the only source of light, casting golden halos across the stone walls, their flames dancing slowly, as if reluctant to let the evening end.

Outside, the world had grown completely still.

Even the usual hum of the night—the rustle of animals settling, the murmurs of neighbours, the cry of a distant trader—had faded into a kind of sacred quiet. Only the faint chirping of night insects and the occasional echo of far-off footsteps remained.

It was as though all of Jericho had paused—breathed in—and remembered.

Eliab's voice rose, low and sure, cutting through the silence not like a disruption, but like the lighting of another lamp. He recited the *Shema*, the oldest words Abner knew—older than bread, older than cities, older than the olive trees along the road.

"Shema Yisrael, Adonai Eloheinu, Adonai Echad..."

Hear, O Israel: The Lord our God, the Lord is One.

The words filled the room with quiet gravity, as if time itself bowed in reverence. Abner closed his eyes, letting the syllables wash over him. He had heard them since he was small enough to fit in a basket by the door, swaddled beside the grinding stone.

But tonight... tonight, the words didn't just pass through him.

They landed.

They settled into his chest like a seed pressing into soil—small, firm, full of promise. Not heavy, but *real*. As if something had been planted in him the moment the sun set and was now beginning to take root.

When the prayers ended, the silence remained. Not empty—never empty—but full of something ancient and tender.

Eliab turned toward him.

There was no urgency in his movement, no demand in his voice. Just invitation.

"My son," he said, his tone quiet but clear, "tell me… what have you learned today?"

Abner hesitated, the question sitting in the stillness like a single fig on a bare branch.

He glanced at his hands, now clean, but still faintly scented with flour and dough. He turned to his mother, who was gently rocking Hila against her shoulder, humming under her breath. Then he looked to the centre of the table, where a single lamp still burned—its small flame rising and falling like a breath. A flicker of life in the quiet.

He opened his mouth, then closed it again.

Then he tried once more.

"I think…" he began, carefully choosing each word, "I think everything takes time. Like the bread. Like the tree."

He paused. The air around him seemed to lean in.

"Like… waiting for the Messiah."

The silence that followed was not stunned, nor tense.

It was *holy*.

Naamah stopped humming. Hila stilled in her arms. The lamp flame gave a tiny sigh.

Eliab's brows lifted—not in alarm, but in something closer to awe. His gaze met Abner's, and for a moment, father and son sat in a silence that spoke louder than any psalm.

Then Eliab smiled. Slowly. Deeply.

A smile that seemed to say, *You've begun to understand.*

And the flame on the table burned on steadier than before.

"You are learning well, my son," Eliab said softly, his voice nearly lost in the quiet crackle of the oil lamp.

Abner sat up a little straighter, his spine lengthening, as though the words had given him height. His eyes, wide and searching, reflected the flame.

"Do you think…" he began, then hesitated, his voice catching like a child holding something fragile. "Do you think we will ever see Him?"

Eliab turned slightly toward him. "Who?" he asked gently, though his eyes already knew. They always had.

Abner looked down, then lifted his gaze again, emboldened by the silence that welcomed his question.

"The Messiah," he said, the word breaking from his lips like a spark struck from flint. "You said God has promised… you've said He will come. That He will make things right."

The room held its breath.

Eliab turned his gaze to Naamah, who sat now with Hila asleep against her chest, her breath slow and steady. Something passed between them—unspoken, but real. It was more than a look. It was a thread pulled tight between memory and longing. Between what had been passed down and what had not yet come.

It was hope.

And it was ache.

Naamah was the one to speak. Her voice, when it came, was both soft and strong—woven like cloth pulled from the loom.

"A tree takes time to grow, Abner," she said, her eyes resting gently on him. "But so does a heart. And your heart... is growing strong."

Abner didn't reply.

He leaned once more against his father's shoulder. Eliab didn't move, only placed his hand lightly across his son's back.

The lamp's glow flickered against the stone wall, casting long shadows that danced like children at play—carefree, joyful, innocent. The air held the weight of peace, like the house itself had exhaled.

Abner let the warmth of the moment settle into him—deeper than skin, deeper than thought. It wrapped itself around something sacred in him and stayed.

This Shabbat felt different.

Not just a pause in the week, not merely a day of rest—but something older.

A remembering.

A rehearsing.

A promise.

A promise of God's faithfulness, His provision... and His coming voice.

And somewhere outside—beyond the walls of their home, beyond the light of the lamps, beneath the cool hush of the evening soil—a tiny seed rested under the watch of stars, waiting. Waiting like they were. Waiting with hope stitched into its silence. Waiting for the warmth to return, for the soil to shift, and for God's voice to whisper, 'Now.'

And one day, when the time was right, without sound or spectacle, it would break the earth.

And stretch toward the light.

Chapter Four:
The Curious Gardener

The rain had come in the night—quietly, steadily, like a whispering visitor slipping through the darkness without fanfare. It hadn't thundered or poured. It had simply arrived, soft as breath, falling in silver threads that gently softened the sharp edges of the world.

By morning, the land had changed.

When Abner stirred beneath his woollen blanket, the first thing he noticed was the air. It was cooler now, touched with a freshness that made him draw in a deep, contented breath. The dryness that had lingered for weeks was gone. In its place was something clean and living, scented with damp earth, olive bark, and the faint herbal sharpness of crushed leaves. The dust that had once clung stubbornly to every surface, every step, had been transformed—darkened, deepened, as if the soil itself had finally exhaled after holding its breath too long.

Abner blinked away the film of sleep from his eyes, his lashes heavy with rest. He stretched his arms above his head, joints gently cracking, and let out a long yawn that curled up from his chest. Morning light, soft and golden, slipped through the woven linen hanging across the window, casting dappled patterns on the stone wall. The fabric shifted with the breeze, cool and clean, stirring like a sigh. It brushed lightly against his face, and he smiled, breathing it in.

The scent of newness. Of renewal. Of a world washed clean.

| *Planted for a purpose*

It was the morning after Shabbat—the first day of the week. The day when tools were lifted again, fires rekindled for labour, and feet began to stir dust on the roads once more.

Yesterday had been filled with stillness—blessings and bread, oil lamps and quiet prayers, the laughter of children and the rustle of linen as hands passed food and affection across the table.

But now... the stillness had passed.

The peace of Shabbat had folded itself like a memory into the heart of the house, and in its place came something different. Not noisy. Not rushed. But full of movement.

The world was stirring again, like a garden waking under rain... and Abner was ready to rise with it. His thoughts snapped to one thing: the seed.

His breath caught, and before his mind could catch up to his body, his feet were already in motion. He threw back the blanket, sprang from his mat, and landed on the cool stone floor with a soft slap. He moved instinctively—barefoot, curls wild with sleep, heart pounding not with fear, but with hope.

The moment the wooden door creaked open beneath his eager hands, a rush of damp morning air met him like a greeting. He darted through the threshold and out into the open, the hush of dawn still clinging to the world like a cloak.

The ground squished slightly beneath his feet, softened by the night's gentle rain. The familiar dirt path, usually dry and chalky, now held the cool memory of water, dark and tender beneath his toes.

The olive trees that lined the way shimmered in the early light, their silver-green leaves dripping with dewdrops. Each droplet clung to the branches like a jewel—fragile, fleeting, and full of beauty. The trees themselves seemed to stretch more fully toward the sun, their gnarled limbs refreshed by the rainfall.

Above him, birds stirred from their nests, singing soft, tentative songs that broke the silence like blessings. Their wings fluttered as they shook off sleep and welcomed the cool hush of the new day—grateful, it seemed, for the rain after so many weeks of unrelenting heat.

Abner's feet barely made a sound as he ran along the path, the sounds of the morning rushing past him in quiet chorus. His pulse quickened as he neared the spot. He slowed only when the patch of earth came into view.

He dropped to his knees beside it, crouching low, the same way he had when he first cradled the seed in his hands. The memory was sharp—his father's voice, his mother's laughter inside, the moment his small fingers had pressed life into the soil.

He stared hard at the ground, his eyes narrowing, his body held still with anticipation. His heart beat loudly in his ears.

Come on, he whispered inwardly. *Show me.*

He leaned closer.

Nothing.

Not a sliver of green. Not the faintest curl of a sprout. No break in the soil. No movement. Only the darkened patch of earth—wet, silent, undisturbed.

It looked the same as it had the day before.

The same as it had the moment he'd covered the seed and whispered his breathless blessing over it.

Still.

Hidden.

Quiet.

And for a moment, Abner's hope wavered—not entirely—but just enough to feel the weight of *waiting* again. His shoulders slumped as disappointment settled in his chest like a small stone.

"Come on," he muttered, frustration edging his voice. "You had rain."

He leaned in closer, so near that the tip of his nose nearly brushed the earth. His eyes scanned the surface for anything— a crack, a swelling, the slightest bulge that might betray life pushing upward. A sign that the seed had heard the rain. That it had listened. That it was coming.

The soil remained as it had been—quiet, unbroken, indifferent.

Abner sat back on his heels and cast a glance over his shoulder. The house stood behind him, still and silent, wrapped in the hush of early morning. No sign of his father. No movement behind the linen curtains. No shadow stretched across the doorway.

His gaze returned to the patch of earth, and something stirred in him—a mix of guilt and determination. He bit his lip, glanced around once more, and lowered himself to the ground.

With one small finger, he pressed into the soil—gently at first. The earth was soft beneath his touch, still damp from the rain, crumbly like honey cake left too long on the table. He pushed a little further, searching for resistance. For the hardness of the seed. For proof it was still there.

But it remained hidden.

Maybe... maybe it had sunk deeper, he reasoned. *Maybe the rain pushed it down too far. Maybe it's stuck. Maybe it needs help.*

The thought burned hotter the longer he looked.

Abner reached for a small stick resting nearby, half-buried beneath a tangle of wet grass. He gripped it tightly and began to dig, carefully at first, as if the earth might forgive a gentle intrusion. He swept the surface, like brushing crumbs from a stone table, moving the soil aside in slow strokes.

But nothing surfaced.

So, he dug a little deeper, searching.

Then deeper still.

His brow furrowed, and his breath quickened. His hands, now streaked with mud, worked faster, more desperately. Each movement was more frantic than the last, as though urgency alone could summon the miracle he longed for.

Please, he thought. *Just let me see it.*

And then—

"Abner!"

The voice struck the air like a stone dropped into still water.

It was deep but not angry.

And somehow, that made it worse. The voice didn't rise in volume. It didn't lash, it didn't accuse.

It was calm. Steady. Strong.

And in its calmness, it carried the weight of something greater than scolding—disappointment wrapped in love. The kind of voice that made the truth impossible to escape. The kind that came not to punish, but to correct.

Abner froze mid-dig, the stick wedged in the dirt, his tunic stained with streaks of wet soil.

His chest tightened. And slowly, he turned toward the voice he knew too well.

Eliab stood a few paces away, arms folded, his expression unreadable. A single eyebrow arched in a way that needed no words.

Abner swallowed hard, his heart thudding fast inside his chest like a bird trying to escape a cage. His father stepped forward

Planted for a purpose

slowly, each movement deliberate, his sandals brushing the damp ground with a soft, scraping sound. Though he said nothing yet, his presence alone filled the space between them, like a shadow passing across the sun, cool and undeniable.

"What exactly," Eliab asked, slightly breathless, annunciating every syllable with exaggerated clarity, "are you doing?"

Abner turned, the stick still clenched awkwardly in his muddy fingers, guilt written across his face like ink on parchment—dark, messy, and impossible to hide. He scratched the back of his head, smearing a streak of brown through his curls without even noticing.

"I... um... I thought maybe..." he stammered, eyes darting toward the hole. "The seed got lost?"

For a moment, Eliab was silent. Abner braced himself, uncertain whether his father was about to laugh, scold, or sigh in that tired way that was heavier than words.

Instead, Eliab crouched down beside him, his knees cracking softly with age, accompanied by a gentle groan. "The seed... got... lost?" he repeated slowly, his voice puzzled and curious, as though tasting the idea, trying to restrain the laughter rising behind his words in that uniquely fatherly way.

Abner nodded earnestly, his face still flushed. "Or maybe it needed help," he added. "I waited yesterday, and I thought... well... the rain came. But nothing has happened."

He gestured toward the hole in the ground, his hand flinging a little mud as frustration bled into his tone—frustration and, perhaps, a trace of accusation. "It's taking too long, Abba."

Eliab didn't respond right away. Then, slowly, deliberately, he reached down and scooped a handful of thick, muddy earth. Without ceremony, he plopped it directly into Abner's outstretched palm.

"Abba!" Abner yelped, eyes going wide as the cold mud squelched between his fingers. "That's disgusting!"

The mud oozed through the gaps in his hand, sticky and wet, clinging to his skin like a living thing.

Eliab chuckled, the sound low and warm, as he reached out and ruffled his son's hair with his right hand, smearing a fresh streak of mud into Abner's already untidy curls.

"The seed is exactly where it should be, my son," he said, his voice gentle but firm. "It does not need your help." He looked at Abner with quiet amusement. "You are so much like our ancestor, Jacob. He, too, would pray to God, asking Him to help with the situation he was facing... and then he would do everything in his own strength to 'help' God—as if God needed his assistance."

Abner scowled at the small hole in front of him, his face clouded with frustration. "But it's just... sitting there in the dirt!" he cried, a slight tear slipping from the corner of his eye. "How does it even know what to do?"

Eliab's smile softened, his amusement giving way to something more profound. He sat back on his heels and rested his hands on his knees, his eyes distant with thought.

"Do you remember what happened when Joshua and the Israelites came across the Jordan to Jericho?"

Abner frowned, unsure what this had to do with his seed. "They walked around the city," he said slowly. "A lot."

"Every day, for six days," Eliab replied, nodding. "And on the seventh day, they walked around the city seven times. And then at Joshua's command, they shouted. And then the walls fell."

Abner tilted his head. "Why didn't they just shout on the first day?"

Eliab's eyes twinkled, his face lit with quiet delight. "Exactly."

Abner blinked. "Wait... what?"

"They followed God's timing," Eliab explained. "Even when it didn't make sense. They had to walk and wait, each day wondering if anything was changing. They had to trust that God was working behind the walls... even when nothing looked different from where they walked and looked."

Abner let out a heavy sigh and flopped back onto the damp grass, his arms spread wide as if surrendering to the sky. The blades, cool and wet beneath him, pressed gently against his back.

"Waiting is so hard," he groaned, his voice muffled by the open air.

Eliab leaned over and gave his son's chest a light pat with the palm of his hand. "It is," he agreed, his tone quiet but steady. "But faith means trusting in what we do not and cannot see. Not just when it's easy... but especially when it's not. That's when we have the greatest faith."

They sat in silence.

The kind of silence that didn't need to be filled.

Above them, the sun rose slowly, spilling its gold across the fields and warming the edges of the world. Birds chirped high in the olive branches, their songs weaving together like morning psalms. Somewhere behind them, a rooster crowed into the breeze, announcing what the sun had already begun.

The world was awakening.

Abner pushed himself up, brushing wet grass from his elbows. His eyes drifted back to the patch of disturbed soil. He picked up the small stick lying nearby and began, quietly and carefully, to refill the hole he had made—sweeping the loose earth back over the place where the seed still lay hidden.

This time, he pressed it down more gently.

With purpose.

With care.

Eliab watched in silence, nodding once, slow and approving.

When the hole was covered once more, Abner stood and wiped his muddy hands down the front of his tunic. Dark streaks followed his fingers, smearing the linen like rough war paint.

He looked up, caught his father's eye, and froze.

Eliab said nothing, but the tilt of his brow told an entire story of disapproval. And yet, the loving smile curling beneath it softened the lesson.

Abner grinned sheepishly in return. "Maybe Hila needs a hug from her big brother?"

Eliab burst into laughter, his whole chest shaking. "Come inside, you muddy little Israelite. Your *ima* will have something to say about this. You and I are very much going to be in trouble."

Abner groaned in mock despair, dragging his feet dramatically. But he followed, trailing behind his father toward the house, leaving behind a line of damp, bare footprints pressed into the dark morning soil.

As soon as they stepped inside, a gasp echoed sharply across the room.

"Abner!"

Naamah stood frozen mid-step, hands planted firmly on her hips. Her eyes scanned her son from head to toe—his wild, mud-streaked curls, the dirt caked beneath his nails and blackening his bare feet. Her expression hovered between disbelief and maternal dread.

"What," she asked, each word precise, "have you done to your clothes?"

Abner opened his mouth to reply, but no words came.

Planted for a purpose

Eliab stepped in smoothly, a calming smile on his face as he reached to take his wife's hand with a familiar, disarming gentleness.

"It's alright, *ahuvati*," he said soothingly. "Our son merely wished to see how much the seed had grown."

Naamah blinked, caught between confusion and rising suspicion. "He... *dug it up?*"

Eliab nodded solemnly. "With the greatest of care."

Naamah turned slowly to face Abner, her gaze narrowing. "That seed will die of shock before it even sees daylight."

Abner winced, his eyes wide with alarm. "I was going to put it back..."

Naamah sighed—a deep, layered breath filled with equal parts exasperation and affection. She crouched beside him, taking the edge of her apron and wiping a streak of mud from his cheek. Her expression was still stern, but her eyes held warmth, the kind that couldn't be faked.

"Go and wash, my son," she said quietly. "I will clean your garment."

She paused, her gaze sharpening as she lowered her voice with meaning. "And no more digging up that seed. Let God do His work... and I will find work for *you* to do, so you don't try to do *His* work again."

Abner grinned, sheepish and unrepentant, nodding quickly as he began backing toward the door that led to the small stone washing basin outside. But just as he reached for the curtain, a sound stopped him.

Giggling.

He turned.

There, near the loom, sat Hila—her legs tucked beneath her, her eyes wide with delight. She covered her mouth with both hands, her curls bouncing as her body shook with laughter she couldn't quite contain.

A playful idea bloomed in Abner's mind like a spark on dry kindling.

Without a word, he crept toward Hila and, with exaggerated drama, swept her into the air. She squealed with delight, her feet dangling as he spun her gently in his arms.

Naamah's voice rose like thunder cracking across a clear sky. "Don't you—!"

Abner froze mid-spin, caught red-handed—literally—his muddy arms wrapped around his now airborne sister.

"She is *clean*," Naamah warned, her eyes narrowing, "and she will *stay* that way."

Hila, unfazed and bubbling with joy, reached up and patted both palms against Abner's mud-streaked cheeks, giggling at the squish and mess of it.

Abner sighed—a long sigh—and gently lowered her back to the mat, her little hands clinging to him until the very last second.

But before he let go, he bent down and brought his face close to hers, his voice dropping to a whisper meant only for her ears.

"Don't worry, Hila," he said softly. "The tree will grow one day. I promise. And you'll be able to climb it. I can't wait to show you."

Hila clapped her hands with glee, eyes bright, entirely unaware of the fresh smear of dirt now adorning her cheek like a badge of honour.

Naamah groaned. "What am I going to do with you?" she muttered, though the corner of her mouth twitched against her will.

Eliab stepped forward, laughter in his eyes as he placed a firm hand on his son's shoulder. "Go, my muddy little gardener," he said, giving him a light push in the direction of the door. "Before your *ima* finds even more work for you and me to do."

Abner darted off with a grin, disappearing toward the washing area. Moments later, the sound of splashing filled the courtyard as he plunged his arms into the stone basin, water sloshing over the sides in gleeful protest. A linen cloth fluttered nearby, stirred gently by the breeze. Abner dried his hands quickly, then dashed back inside, ready to create mischief once again with Hila.

And as the morning sun climbed higher, brightening the sky above Jericho with golden clarity, a small patch of soil in their yard sat quiet and undisturbed once more—its surface smooth, its secret hidden. Beneath that humble mound lay a treasure, unseen but not forgotten, cradled in the dark by the patient hands of providence.

It was waiting.

Waiting for the right time.

The appointed time.

To break the earth.

To rise.

Chapter Five:
The Marketplace and the Fig Seller

The mid-morning air in Jericho buzzed with life. Sunlight cascaded over the sandstone buildings, casting long, slanted shadows that danced across winding alleys and courtyards. The scent of freshly baked bread mingled with the sharp tang of pickled olives, crushed herbs, and roasting fish, wrapping the marketplace in a heady, mouth-watering perfume. The city didn't merely stir—it pulsed, alive with colour, heat, and noise.

Abner walked contentedly beside his mother; his small hand curled loosely around the edge of her tunic as they threaded their way through the press of bodies and baskets. His sandaled feet scuffed up swirls of fine, golden dust that glittered in the sun. From every corner, voices clashed and tangled—shouting, bartering, calling, laughing. Doves wheeled and flapped from rooftop to rooftop in nervous bursts. Pottery clinked with the sound of commerce. Bundles of dyed wool shifted in baskets as sellers displayed their wares with flourish and aplomb. The marketplace surged like a river, restless and relentless—teeming with human life, animal cries... and something more. Something just beneath the surface.

He had walked these streets with his *ima* many times. Yet the rhythm, the rush, the energy of the market never lost its magic.

Still... today, something felt different.

"If only I were taller," Abner thought with a flicker of frustration,

Planted for a purpose

shifting from foot to foot as he tried to peer over the shoulders of the bustling crowd. Voices swelled around him, and though he could hear the numerous sounds of wonder and barter, the sights remained just out of reach. "Then I could see all the things I hear."

The market stalls stretched along both sides of the street, their faded canvas canopies snapping in the breeze like sails above a sea of bodies. Vendors leaned forward with outstretched arms and persuasive smiles, their voices rising above the din like temple preachers calling worshippers to repentance. Each one peddled treasure and tale—each one reaching for a buyer, a coin, an ear.

"Fine linens! Straight from Jerusalem!"

"Spices! Cinnamon, myrrh, cardamom—come, smell the riches of the East!

"Figs!"

The single word rang out—not louder than the others, but different. Far clearer. Like the single tone of a bell, distinct and apparent. It didn't shout. It struck.

Abner froze. Something in the voice stirred him, quiet and confident, as though it hadn't spoken to the crowd at all—but to him alone.

He turned quickly, eyes scanning the crowd, his gaze jumping from face to face, brow furrowed in wonder.

Where did that come from?

His gaze landed on a modest wooden stall silently tucked between two larger, bustling ones, where customers jostled each other. But the quiet stall, no one looked or lingered. Yet there, arranged in woven baskets and sun-warmed clay bowls, lay a mountain of figs—deep purple, golden brown, some nearly bursting at the seams. Their wrinkled skins whispered of delicious sweetness within, and they glistened in the morning light like scattered gemstones waiting to be found.

Naamah had paused at the grain stall a few paces back, deep in negotiation with a merchant over measures of barley and lentils. Usually, Abner would have lingered to watch. His mother's skill at haggling was legendary—she could dismantle a vendor's price with a single lifted eyebrow and a well-timed sigh, or the quick appearance of turning to walk away.

But not today.

Today, something else had captured him.

"Fresh pomegranates and figs!"

There it was again—that same voice. Not loud. Not urgent. But unmistakably *directed*. As if spoken through the crowd, not into it.

Compelled by the scent and the sound, Abner drifted toward the fig stall, his sandals whispering against the dust. His body seemed to move before his mind had caught up. He stopped just short of the baskets, his fingers twitching with the instinct to reach out. The figs looked soft and heavy with juice, their surfaces glistening as though each one held the breath of the sun. There was a strange vibrancy to them. They didn't just *look* ripe.

They looked alive.

A low, amused chuckle rumbled from behind the table.

"You have an eye for good fruit, young one."

Abner jumped slightly, blinking, and looked up.

An elderly man sat behind the stall, perched on a low wooden stool. His skin was deeply weathered, creased by years of sun and wind; his beard, long and white, framed his face like a fringe of wool spun silver. Aged hands rested atop a carved wooden staff, the wood worn smooth by time. But it was his eyes that held Abner—sharp,

Planted for a purpose

clear, and unsettlingly knowing, as though they had seen far more than a life's worth of days should allow.

Abner hesitated, then gave a slight nod. "They look... perfect."

The man smiled, and deep furrows crinkled around his eyes like folds in old parchment. He reached for a fig from the top of the pile and turned it thoughtfully in his hand. "Thank you, Abner. You should try this one," he said, offering it gently. "It's full of flavour. You can always tell—when the skin begins to soften just so."

He paused, his gaze sharpening slightly.

"Do you know how long it takes for a fig tree to bear good fruit?"

Abner frowned, his thoughts jumping instantly to the seed he had pressed into the soil days ago. "A year?"

The old man threw his head back in a rich, rolling laugh—not mocking, but full of warmth, like one who had heard the question a hundred times and never tired of answering it.

"Oh, if only! No, no, young one. A sycamore fig tree takes years before it yields fruit worth tasting. Years of sinking its roots deep, of thickening its trunk, of stretching its arms toward the sky."

Abner's shoulders slumped. Days had passed with no sign—no shoot, no bud, not even a crack in the soil. The seed he had planted remained buried... hidden... silent.

The fig seller narrowed his eyes slightly, studying the boy as if reading a scroll. "You look troubled, lad."

Abner cast a glance over his shoulder toward the grain stall. His mother was still deep in discussion with the merchant, her hands slicing the air with conviction.

"I planted a tree," Abner said at last, the words escaping before he could question why. There was something about the old man's voice—steady, quiet—that made honesty feel easy. "But... It's taking too long."

The old man gave a slow, knowing nod, both hands resting on his staff like an elder ready to teach a well-worn lesson.

"Ah, I see," he said. "You're like a farmer who plants a seed and expects a harvest by sunrise."

Abner shrugged. "It's rained. I've watered it. I keep checking it. And even though it's been a few weeks…" Abner paused midsentence. He lowered his gaze. "I even… sort of… dug it up again."

The vendor raised his eyebrows, smiled kindly and knowingly, but remained silent.

Abner shifted his weight, scraping the sole of his sandal against the dusty stone. "I just wanted to see if anything was happening."

The old man leaned forward slightly, his voice softer now, like the hush before dawn. "Tell me—how does a tree know when to grow?"

Abner blinked, unsure how to answer. "I don't know. It just… does?"

"Exactly," the man said with a nod. "Because God tells it to. Just as He tells the sun when to rise, the clouds when to give rain, and the stars when to shine. He tells the plants of the field when to grow."

Abner looked up at him, puzzled, but something about the words stirred him. There was mystery in them. And truth.

"The tree is growing already," the man continued, his voice like slow-poured honey. "But not where you can see it… yet. Growth begins subtly in the dark, where the roots begin to stretch deep, anchoring the tree firmly and properly. If it reached for the sky before finding its footing beneath, it would topple with the slightest breeze."

Abner's thoughts turned again to the story of Jericho he had heard from his father. The circling. The silence. The waiting. The trust.

"But what if something happens to it?" he asked, the worry slipping into his tone. "What if it dies? What if I waited for nothing?"

Planted for a purpose

The man lifted a smaller fig from the basket—still green, firm to the touch. Not yet ready.

"A tree appears strong when it is grown," he said, turning the fruit in his hand, "but when it is young, it is tender. Exposed. That's when it needs guarding and protecting. Sunlight to warm it. Soil to hold it. And time—always time."

He paused, his gaze meeting Abner's eyes, and intent in his tone now, "And it needs a gardener."

Abner's brow furrowed in thought. "So... I have to protect it as it grows?"

"Yes," the man responded with a slightly emphatic tone. "As a shepherd watches over his flock through night and storm, as well as from the predator, so too must a gardener tend his soil to protect his planting."

Abner straightened, a quiet determination in his voice. "How? How can a gardener do all that?"

The old man's smile deepened. He tapped the ground lightly with the end of his staff.

"Keep the earth soft and watered. Soil must be made ready, or nothing takes root. It is hidden now, safely beneath the surface, out of reach from the birds who snatch what falls exposed along the path. That you have done correctly already, guard it from careless feet that trample without thought and from the harsh sunlight. If it sprouts from the ground and the roots have not spread deeply enough, it will shrivel as it burns. Finally, uproot every thorn and creeping weed that would steal strength from the plant. It would still grow, but the growth would be hampered, and the tree would never reach its full potential. Then—only then—can the seed grow deep in good soil." He leaned in slightly, eyes glinting with quiet mischief. "And above all...

learn to wait."

Abner groaned, half-smiling. "Everyone keeps saying that to me. Especially Abba."

The stall vendor chuckled, low and knowing. "Because it is the only way to see what's coming."

Just then, a familiar voice rang out behind him.

"Abner?"

He turned. Naamah stood a few stalls away, balancing a sack of grain under one arm, her eyes sweeping the street in search of him.

"I have to go," Abner said quickly, stepping back from the stall.

But the fig seller extended his hand and pressed the ripe fruit into Abner's palm. "Take this," he said, voice warm. "Come back and see me when your tree grows."

Abner tucked the fig into the fold of his tunic, offered a grateful smile, and turned to go.

"Abner?" his mother called again, looking at him puzzled, her voice carrying over the hum of the marketplace, yet with a tone of slight confusion.

He walked quickly back to her side, his hand brushing against the fruit beneath his tunic. Naamah gave him a brief, questioning glance but said nothing. She placed her hand gently on his back, and together they continued through the winding path of stalls.

But Abner couldn't help himself. After a few steps, he looked back.

The stall was still there.

But the man...

The man was gone.

No stool. No staff. No figs.

A thought came—seemingly from nowhere, but certain. The man knew my name.

Planted for a purpose

He looked back again.

Nothing there. Just the empty stall.

Abner frowned, the weight of it settling slowly, like dust drifting down upon a forgotten path.

I never told him, Abner thought, all the more puzzled.

But he called me by name.

And though the air was thick once more with voices and smells and sunlight, only the echo of that voice remained, lingering like the scent of honey on the breeze.

Not loud.

Not urgent.

But planted deep.

Abner placed his hand against his tunic hesitantly and tentatively, feeling the teardrop shape of the fig still safely tucked away in the folds.

Chapter Six:
The First Sign of Life

The sun hung lower in the sky, painting the buildings of Jericho in a warm amber hue as Abner and Naamah made their way home late in the afternoon. The heat of the day had begun to wane, and the dust beneath their feet no longer shimmered with heat but settled quietly, coating their sandals in a fine rust-coloured powder.

The busy noise of the market had faded behind them, replaced by gentler sounds—the distant braying of donkeys, the soft sweep of a broom against stone, and the bright laughter of children darting between doorways and courtyards, their games weaving familiar patterns through the quiet streets of the outer town.

Naamah walked steadily, the basket of grain balanced against her hip. Her breathing was calm, her gaze forward, steady with purpose. Abner walked slightly behind, one hand tucked into the fold of his tunic, his fingers curled protectively around the fig the old vendor had given him.

But it wasn't the fruit he clung to—it was the words.

A tree looks strong when it is grown... but when it is young, it needs care, patience, and protection.

The echo of that voice lingered—not in his ears, but deep in his spirit.

Abner replayed those words again and again, as though each repetition might somehow coax the tree to grow faster. Would it really grow? Would it one day stand tall enough to climb? Would it bear fruit—sweet and golden, like the ones he had seen glistening at the market stall? The thought of it—of a tree that was his—made his chest swell with a quiet, hopeful pride.

They rounded the final bend in the path, the sun slipping gently behind the hills.

Their small stone house came into view, and beside it, the garden.

They walked a little further, and that's when Abner stopped.

Dead in his tracks.

His eyes widened.

His breath caught in his throat.

There, rising from the earth like a secret unveiled, was the tiniest sprout. Just a sliver of green—no longer than the tip of his finger—breaking bravely through the soil where only weeks ago he had pressed the seed into the dirt.

It was fragile. Almost nothing. But it was there.

Alive.

It's growing, he thought to himself, wonder bursting within him like light.

"Ima!" he gasped, pointing with breathless excitement. "Look!"

Naamah turned, following his gaze. A smile softened her features as she took in the sight.

"Ah," she said, her voice rich with warmth, "so the waiting was not for nothing, hmm?"

Abner dropped to his knees beside the tiny sprout. He hovered over it, mouth parted in awe. It looked so delicate—like it might vanish with a single breath—yet it stood bravely, its slender stem reaching toward the sky with all the courage the earth could muster.

His tree.

The seed he had planted.

Something stirred in him—deeper than joy, more tender than surprise. It was reverence as though he were witnessing a prayer unfurling before his eyes.

Gently, he reached out, his fingers hovering just above the fragile shoot. He didn't touch it. He didn't dare. It was too new. Too sacred.

Then, almost without meaning to, he whispered, "You are a special tree."

His voice barely rose above the wind.

"You don't know it yet, but one day... people will see you. You will grow tall and strong, and maybe children will climb your branches. Maybe travellers will rest in your shade."

He paused, realising he sounded just like his abba.

"You are my special tree," he whispered again, smiling gleefully at the sprout.

A warm breeze stirred the olive tree branches nearby, and the sprout quivered gently in response. Abner grinned again.

He leapt to his feet and bolted toward the house, heart pounding with excitement. The fig tucked in his pocket bounced against his hip as he ran.

"Abba! Abba! Come quick!"

Inside, Eliab sat at the table, trimming a worn leather sandal strap. He looked up sharply at the urgency in his son's voice.

"What is it, my son?"

Naamah entered just behind Abner, setting down her basket with a shake of her head and an amused smile.

Eliab's brow eased. This wasn't fear. This was sheer joy.

Abner grabbed his father's hand with both of his, tugging. "Come see! The tree—our tree—it's growing!"

| *Planted for a purpose*

Eliab rose slowly, a quiet smile forming as he allowed himself to be led toward the door.

Abner raced ahead, while Eliab followed at his own pace, slower than usual, walking with quiet expectation toward the outer garden.

Abner once again crouched beside the sprout, Eliab following more slowly, settling beside him with his strong hands resting on his knees. He leaned in close, eyes tracing the slender stem.

"It has begun, then," he said softly to his son.

Abner nodded, beaming. "Look at it!"

Eliab nodded again, his voice low. "It is good."

Abner's heart swelled, fit to burst with pride.

Then, as if suddenly remembering, he reached into his tunic and pulled out the fig.

"Abba, at the market, there was this man… an old man at the fig stall. He talked to me about trees. About how they take time. How they need to be protected."

Eliab took the fig from his son's hand, turning it slowly in his palm. He examined it not just as fruit, but as though it carried a message.

"So, he told you what I told you?" Eliab said with a small smile. "Sometimes the same truth must be spoken twice before we hear it. What else did he say?"

Abner thought for a moment. "He said… a tree looks strong when it's grown. But when it's young, it needs a lot of care."

Eliab nodded, and for a moment, his face grew thoughtful—almost distant. "The man at the market spoke very wisely."

He placed a hand gently on Abner's shoulder.

"If you want this tree to grow strong, you must guard it like a shepherd watches and protects his flock. Like a father watches over his family. Like the firstborn with the birthright."

Abner's eyes lit with determination. "I will. I'll sleep outside tonight if I have to."

Eliab laughed—a rich, kind sound that warmed the space between them.

"No, my son. Not that. God tends to creation, yes—but He calls us to tend it too. Feed it. Water it. Watch the soil. Keep the weeds away. Speak to it if you must. And when the storms come—and they will—stand nearby."

Abner grinned and turned back to the sprout. His heart thudded with a kind of love he hadn't known he could feel for something so small.

Eliab rose and surveyed the area thoughtfully. "Let's collect some small stones. We'll circle them around the sprout, so no one steps on it by mistake. And so you'll know exactly where to look each day, though I suspect you'd find it even with your eyes shut." He chuckled.

Abner leapt into action, scanning the outer garden for pebbles and placing them gently in a ring around the shoot. He chose each stone with care, brushing off the dirt with his fingers and pressing them softly into the soil. His movements were slow, deliberate, almost ceremonial.

Eliab joined him in silence, placing one final stone to complete the protective circle around the fragile sprout.

Slightly breathless, Eliab said to Abner, "Now give it some water from the jug."

Abner bolted toward the side of the house and returned moments later with a small clay cup. He knelt again and tilted it carefully, letting a thin trickle of water run down the tender shoot and into the waiting soil.

The earth darkened beneath it, drinking deeply.

Planted for a purpose

Abner stared at the sprout, then leaned in close, his voice soft as a breath. "Grow strong, little tree."

Eliab stood behind him, arms folded, watching. A quiet joy rose in his chest, steady and full. But there was something else beneath it.

He reached out and gently patted Abner's head. "You've planted more than a tree, my son," he said. "You've planted a lesson in life. And I believe the Lord sees."

Abner looked up, eyes shining. "You really think so?"

Eliab smiled. "I don't think, this I know."

Chapter Seven:
Do Not Listen to Doubt

It was early morning when Abner crouched beside his tree, carefully brushing away the tiniest speck of dust that had settled on one of its delicate leaves. The wind from the night before had come howling down from the nearby mountains, sweeping through the narrow streets of Jericho and rattling the thatched rooftops—layers of mud and straw now flecked with debris. He had lain awake in the dark, listening to the groaning timbers and the cries of the wind, fearing the worst for his fragile sapling. But despite the storm, the little tree had endured.

It stood now, small, trembling slightly as though still recovering from the night's assault—but alive.

Reaching.

Stretching.

Becoming.

A few paces away, Hila sat cross-legged on the stone path, watching him with wide, curious eyes. Her dark curls bounced as she tilted her head to one side, mimicking a bird pecking at the ground, then pausing to look up, trying to make sense of what it saw.

Abner glanced over at her and smiled to himself. *She's growing up so quickly,* he thought. *I wish the tree would grow as fast as she does.*

Hila's small voice broke his thoughts. "How come you love it?"

Abner glanced back at the sprout and instinctively cupped his hands around it, shielding it from some invisible threat.

"What? The tree?" he said kindly, unbothered by her question. "Because it's mine, Hila. I planted it, and I promised to take care of it. It's young, and it needs help to grow. Just like you."

He grinned. "You've got a big brother. But the tree doesn't. It's growing here on its own. So even when I'm looking after you,"—he gave her a playful glance—"it reminds me to look after it, too."

Hila wrinkled her nose. "But it's little."

Abner laughed, brushing back his windblown curls. "Not for long."

He ran his fingers gently along the circle of protective stones he and his father had placed. The morning's watering had darkened the soil, and a single droplet clung to the tip of the sprout's leaf—like a tear not yet shed.

Then, without warning, a shadow fell across him.

At first, Abner thought it was a passing cloud. But the presence behind him made the hairs on his neck rise. He felt it more than he saw it.

"That's your tree?" a voice sneered overhead.

Abner turned.

It was Barak.

He was slightly older than Abner, although he was also leaner, faster, and stronger. His dusty tunic hung loose from his frame, and his arms were folded as he loomed with a crooked smirk. His skin was sun-darkened, his eyes sharp with mischief.

Abner rose to his feet. "Yes. It's mine. It's my tree, and it's going to grow big."

Barak snorted. "That?" He nodded toward the sprout with disdain. "That's not a tree. That's a weed. You're wasting your time, Abner."

Heat surged in Abner's chest. "It's not a weed!"

Barak began circling the sprout like a jackal, slow and mocking. "You can't even climb it," he scoffed. "What's the point of a tree that does nothing?"

Hila watched quietly from the path, her fingers clutching the edge of her tunic. She had seen Barak before. He didn't laugh like her brother, and he didn't smile with kindness like him either. There was something in his eyes—hard and mean. Something that didn't care for small things or gentle things.

Without warning, Barak lifted his foot and kicked a wave of dirt over the sprout.

Abner's breath caught.

The little stem vanished beneath a spray of dust.

Something inside him snapped.

With a cry, he lunged forward, shoving Barak with both hands. Barak staggered, surprised—but only for a moment. His face twisted—amusement giving way to fury.

Barak shoved him hard. Abner staggered backwards, his heels catching on a loose rock, causing him to tumble awkwardly, twisting as he fell. His elbow and hip struck the ground first, a sharp jolt of pain shooting through him. Dust billowed in a dry puff, clinging to his tunic and face.

Barak laughed, brushing off his tunic. "You can't even fight. That weed's just like you—small and weak."

Abner's face burned. His fists clenched in the dirt. He could feel the fig in his pocket, pressed firm against his side—as though it, too, remembered.

He was about to leap—

When a voice, stern and unmistakable, sliced through the rising heat of his anger.

"Enough!"

Both boys froze.

Eliab stood a few steps away, resting resolutely on his staff. His posture was calm, but there was steel in his eyes. He looked first at Barak, then at his son lying in the dust.

Barak shifted, suddenly uncertain. He met Eliab's gaze, then turned and ran, kicking up a fresh trail of dust as he disappeared down the lane.

Eliab didn't call after him.

Instead, he stepped forward and knelt beside Abner, setting his staff gently to one side.

"Are you hurt?" he asked softly.

Abner sat up, brushing his dusty palms against his tunic. His knees stung. His pride, more so.

"I'm fine," he muttered.

But he wasn't. His chest was tight. His throat burned. His eyes stung—not with tears, but something worse. Doubt. Shame. Helplessness.

Eliab said nothing at first. He reached forward, brushing the scattered soil away from the circle of stones, then gently wiped the dust from the top of the sprout.

The tiny stem still stood. Bent, slightly scarred—but not broken.

Abner stared. The lump in his throat rose again.

"He said... it'll never grow," he whispered, voice cracking.

Eliab sighed, placing a steady hand on his son's shoulder.

"Let me tell you a story, my son."

Abner glanced up, silent. His fists still clenched tightly.

Eliab shifted lower beside him, crouching until their eyes were level—father and son, knee to knee, heart to heart.

"A long time ago," Eliab began, "after Moses led our people out of Egypt, twelve men were sent to spy out the land of Canaan."

Abner nodded. He knew this story—his abba had told it to him more than once.

"When they returned," Eliab continued, "ten of them were afraid. They said, 'The land is good… but the people there are giants. We can't win.' They convinced the Israelites to believe in fear instead of believing and trusting God."

He paused, letting the silence settle.

"But two, only two—Joshua and Caleb—stood firm. They trusted God, even when everything looked impossible."

Abner glanced down. "But no one listened to them."

"That's right," Eliab said. "The people chose fear. And so, they wandered the wilderness for forty years."

He let the weight of that truth linger.

Then, quietly: "If you start listening to voices that mock what God is growing in you, you'll end up wandering too."

Abner looked up slowly.

"Barak doesn't see what you see," Eliab said gently. "He doesn't know what God is doing here. But you do. Or at least… you want to. And that"—he placed his hand on Abner's chest—"that is faith."

Abner turned back to the sprout. Its slender stem swayed in the breeze, but it still stood.

"It will grow, Abner," Eliab said. "But only if you believe it will. Only if you keep watering it. Guarding it. Trusting the One who made it."

A long silence followed—a knowing pause between father and son. Then came a slight shuffling sound.

Hila stepped forward, her hands outstretched, gently brushing

Planted for a purpose

the last of the soil from the sprout. Her fingers were dusty but careful, her expression fierce with quiet determination.

"It's your tree," she whispered. "It's special to me, too."

Abner blinked. The anger faded—melted into something softer, warmer.

He leaned forward and placed his hand near hers.

Then, once more, like a promise:

"Grow strong, little tree."

He turned and pulled Hila into a hug, holding her tightly. She was small, but her words were brave.

Eliab smiled and reached down to ruffle his son's hair.

"Come inside," he said. "You'll need water for that scrape... and if we're lucky, your Ima won't notice."

Abner stood, dust falling from his tunic. "She'll notice," he said dryly, looking up at his father, hoping for a way out.

Eliab laughed. "Yes, she will."

Together, they walked toward the house, leaving behind a circle of stones and a tiny green sprout.

Behind them, the tree stood steady.

Bent, yes.

But not broken.

Chapter Eight:
The Circle Grows

The morning sun cast long shadows across the garden as Abner knelt beside his tree, his knees pressing into the soft earth worn smooth by months of visits. He leaned forward slightly, his careful gaze absorbing every detail—each leaf, each curve of the slender stem, each new shoot daring to grow. His fingertips traced the rough, sun-warmed stones that ringed the base of the tree, brushing away a thin veil of dust that had gathered overnight.

Above him, a light breeze moved through the olive branches, whispering gently through the leaves and stirring golden notes in the morning air. The garden, usually filled with the low rustle of hens or the far-off call of neighbours, felt still, reverent, as though time itself had paused to honour the quiet miracle before him.

It had been months since he'd knelt here with shaking hope, a fistful of stones, and a pocketed fig. Months since that hushed afternoon with his abba, circling the first fragile sprout and learning the sacred art of waiting.

Back then, it had barely pierced the surface—just a slender green whisper rising from the soil.

But now?

Now, the tree had presence.

Its stem had thickened, no longer delicate or unsure, but beginning to bear the faint ridges and grooves of young bark.

The leaves—broad, deep green, and dappled with morning light—shimmered with life. Veins ran through them like tiny rivers, and when the wind stirred, they flickered like lamp flames.

New shoots extended outward—small but bold—the first sign of branches forming, like arms learning how to stretch toward the heavens.

Still, Abner knew it was young. The roots were not yet deep enough to drink from the earth during drought. A stiff wind could still bend it low. It could be wounded by careless feet or choked by the sly return of weeds.

But it was no longer small.

It no longer looked like doubt.

It looked like promise.

He smiled like a proud father as he ran a finger gently along the edge of one of the leaves. "You're growing," he whispered, his voice soft with wonder.

But then his eyes dropped to the stones.

The circle that had once stood like sentinels around the sprout—his carefully chosen ring of protection—now pressed too closely. The rocks, once guardians against careless feet and trampling weight, had become a kind of barrier. Their closeness no longer offered safety, but restraint.

What had once shielded now threatened to confine.

The smile slowly faded from his face.

"I need to fix this," he muttered, frowning. "But what should I do?"

He rose, brushing the dust from his knees, his back arching in a stretch that caught the warmth of the morning sun. The light shining across his shoulders like a gentle cloak.

"Abba!" he called, his voice rising clearly across the courtyard.

A moment later, Eliab appeared in the doorway, a wooden cup in his hand, trembling ever so slightly with age. Despite the frailty of movement, his expression remained steady, serene even, as though he had already guessed why he'd been summoned.

"Yes, my son?"

Abner gestured urgently toward the tree. "The rocks. They're too close. The tree's getting bigger—I think I need to move them."

Eliab stepped slowly into the garden, each step deliberate, his sandals pressing shallow prints into the softened earth. He approached the tree without speaking at first, letting his gaze travel over its form—the thickened stem, the reaching branches, the circle of stones hugging too tightly around its base.

"Yes," Eliab said with quiet satisfaction. "It is getting much bigger."

He stood beside his son, resting his staff on one of the stones. His voice lowered, almost reverent. "Just like you."

Abner blinked. "Like me?"

Eliab smiled, the lines at the corners of his eyes deepening with warmth. "Yes. You didn't need anyone to tell you to grow—you just did. God placed that knowledge inside you. Just as He did in the tree."

With a gentle push of his staff, Eliab nudged one of the stones. It rolled a little, shifting the shape of the circle. He watched it thoughtfully.

"The seed carried everything it needed," he continued. "It didn't wait for permission. It followed the path God set for it—and it still is."

Abner frowned, brow furrowing in thought. "So... should I take the stones away?"

Eliab shook his head slowly. "Not all of them. It still needs protection. The world hasn't grown softer. But the circle must grow wider, just as your world does as you grow. Safety is not the same as restriction. Give it room to become what it's meant to be."

Abner nodded, dropping to his knees. He began lifting the stones one by one, setting each aside with care. Then, with equal precision, he placed them again—this time wider, roomier, more generous. The tree, it seemed, stood taller already.

Eliab watched in silence, his eyes distant.

Then he cleared his throat. "Did I ever tell you about the twelve stones in the Jordan?"

Abner paused, mid-reach, and looked up. "Twelve stones?"

Eliab nodded slowly. "When Joshua led our people into the Promised Land, they came to the Jordan River during flood season. The waters were high, wild, and impassable. But God held them back—just as He had done with the Red Sea for Moses."

Abner's eyes widened slightly. He had heard of Moses and the sea, of course. But this part of Joshua's story was new to him, and it stirred his imagination.

Eliab continued, leaning gently on his staff, his gaze resting on the stones Abner was now shifting. "When the priests carrying the Ark of the Covenant stepped into the water, the river stopped flowing. And after they crossed, Joshua told one man from each tribe to take a stone from the dry riverbed and carry it to the other side. There, they stacked the twelve stones into a memorial."

Abner paused in his task, tilting his head thoughtfully. "Why did they stack them?"

Eliab smiled. "So that when children came across them and asked, 'What do these stones mean?' they could be told the story—how God held back the waters and brought His people through."

Abner picked up one of the stones and turned it over in his hand, seeing it differently now, not just as a marker, not just as protection.

"A reminder," he whispered, more to himself than anyone.

Eliab nodded, his voice gentle but sure. "Exactly."

Abner looked back at his tree, eyes glinting with new understanding.

"Then I don't just need to protect the tree... I need to remember," he said slowly, as though the thought was still forming. "Remember that it's grown... and that God is the One helping it."

He rose to his feet, the dust of the garden clinging to his knees, his voice stronger now. "I'm going to place twelve stones. Like Joshua. A new circle—not just for safety, but for thankfulness."

Eliab grinned and reached out to ruffle his son's hair, pride warming his weathered features. "That is a very wise thought, my son."

Abner's chest lifted with quiet pride—his heart swelling with something far greater than the task before him.

Hila, who had been watching silently from a few steps away, now appeared beside them, cradling a smooth stone in both hands.

"I found this one," she said matter-of-factly, offering it up to her brother.

Abner smirked. "You're helping again?"

Hila shrugged with innocence. "It's your tree," she replied.

Together, they worked under the watchful gaze of Eliab.

Stone by stone.

They widened the circle, taking care not just to shield what the tree was now, but to make space for what it would one day become.

Each stone was chosen with intention—its shape, its smoothness, how well it nestled beside the others. Their fingers worked through the soil with quiet reverence. And as the new circle slowly took form, something about the tree itself seemed to respond. It stood a little taller, its leaves catching the light with more confidence, as though proud to be honoured.

When the final stone found its place, Eliab stepped back, his staff resting lightly against his leg, and surveyed their work. The sunlight danced through the branches, and a gentle breeze stirred the topmost leaves.

Then Eliab spoke, softly—his voice slowing to the cadence of scripture:

"For you shall go out with joy,
And be led out with peace;
The mountains and the hills
Shall break forth into singing before you,
And all the trees of the field shall clap their hands."

Abner turned to him, brows raised. "Trees can clap?"

Eliab chuckled, eyes glinting. "The prophet Isaiah said so. He was describing joy so great, even the trees would join the celebration."

Abner looked at the leaves, shimmering in the breeze. "Are they praising God already?"

Eliab didn't answer, but the gentle smile on his face said everything.

Abner stepped close to the tree once more and placed his palm gently against the slender stem. It was firmer than before—less fragile, more sure of itself. Steady.

"You will grow strong," he whispered.

Behind him, Hila giggled. "Are you talking to the tree again?"

Abner glanced over his shoulder, grinning. "I think it's listening."

Eliab reached out and placed an arm around his son's shoulders.

"Then let it hear this—God will continue the work He has begun."

Abner's heart stirred at the words.

They felt like a promise. Like a prophecy.

He took Hila's hand in his, and together they began walking toward the house. His feet brushed the dusty earth, but his thoughts soared like birds on the morning breeze.

At the doorway, he paused and turned once more. The tree stood within the widened ring of twelve stones—marked, honoured, and full of future.

And Abner knew.

This tree would one day stand tall, not just for shade, not just for beauty—but as a living sign.

A sign that God had been faithful.

A sign that what starts small, when tended with patience and protected with care, grows into something strong.

Perhaps one day, its branches would stretch wide enough for birds to nest in its arms, for children to laugh in its shade, and for passers-by to pause, not just to rest, but to wonder. And its leaves—stirred by the wind—would clap their hands in silent praise.

And the One who made the seed would smile... And remember the boy who planted it.

Chapter Nine:
Evergreen

Abner strolled through the streets of Jericho, his sandals kicking up crisp, dry leaves scattered across the dusty ground. The soft rustle of their crunching echoed faintly with each step, curling at the edges, their deep green faded to pale yellow and brittle brown.

He frowned. The trees were changing.

All around him, branches once full and leafy were turning bare, their limbs stretched toward the sky, empty and exposed. The fig trees near the market had already lost half their leaves. The olive groves had grown sparse, and the vineyards beyond the city were covered in golden vines, their once-full canopies now shrivelled and scattered across the earth.

Everything is dying, he thought.

A tight knot formed in his stomach.

What about my tree?

His pace quickened, sandals tapping more urgently along the cobbled path. The rhythm of his breathing grew shallow, and his heartbeat thudded in his ears. He had spent months watching it grow, measuring its progress, protecting it from goats, shielding it from the weight of careless feet. What if, after everything, it was beginning to wither like the others?

By the time he reached the courtyard, his breath came in short gasps.

Planted for a purpose

Then he stopped, his heart pounding.

His tree stood tall in its usual place. Still green. Still strong. Not a single leaf had fallen.

Abner stepped forward, cautiously at first, reaching out to touch one of the smooth leaves. It felt the same—alive, vibrant, unchanged.

Confused, he turned toward the side of the courtyard. Eliab sat nearby on a low stool, carefully mending a wooden yoke for the oxen. His father had been watching him, a knowing smile tugging at the corners of his mouth.

"You ran home as if you'd seen an army coming over the hills," Eliab remarked, setting the yoke down.

Abner hesitated, rubbing the back of his neck. "I... I thought maybe the tree was dying."

Eliab raised an eyebrow. "And why did you think that?"

Abner gestured beyond the courtyard. "The other trees. They're losing their leaves. The fig trees, the vines, even the olive trees. But my tree..."

He trailed off, turning back to look at it.

Eliab stood and walked over, motioning for Abner to join him. Together, they knelt beside the young sycamore, the cool shadow of its branches falling over their backs.

"Do you know why your tree has not lost its leaves?" Eliab asked.

Abner shook his head.

Eliab glanced toward the trees beyond their home, where a breeze sent another flurry of golden leaves drifting to the ground.

"Some trees lose their leaves because God has told them to," he said knowingly. "They must let go to survive the colder seasons. That is how they were made. It's part of God's plan for them."

Abner frowned. "But not mine?"

Eliab smiled, resting a hand on his son's shoulder. "No, not yours. Your tree is different. It is evergreen."

Abner's brows furrowed. "Evergreen?"

Eliab nodded. "No matter the season, it will remain standing. Its leaves will always be full, always green. Even when other trees fade, yours will not. That is how God created this type of tree. It is a sycamore."

Abner ran his fingers over one of the thick leaves, relief washing over him.

But another thought quickly followed. Why?

"Why do some trees stay strong while others have to lose everything?" he asked quietly.

Eliab exhaled slowly, studying his son before answering.

"Do you remember the story of Jericho?"

Abner nodded.

"When our people came to this land, the walls of Jericho fell. The great city that had stood for so long came crashing down."

Abner had heard the story many times. The Israelites marched. The trumpets blew. The walls fell.

Eliab's voice softened. "But not all of it fell, did it?"

Abner's head snapped up. "Rahab's house."

Eliab nodded. "Yes. She lived in the most dangerous part of the city—the wall itself. When the city crumbled, the wall should have crumbled too. But her house stood."

Abner's eyes widened. "But why?"

Eliab grew thoughtful. "Rahab was not an Israelite. She was a Canaanite. But when Joshua sent two spies into the city, Rahab took them in and protected them."

He gestured to the distant horizon beyond their home. "Look

beyond the rooftops of Jericho, Abner. Do you see the remains of the old walls?"

Abner followed his father's gaze and spotted the crumbled ruins in the distance—the broken stone, the rubble that had once been mighty fortifications.

Eliab crouched beside him, his voice low and certain.

"She was the first to declare the Lord as the God of heaven above and the earth below. Because she kept the spies safe, she pleaded for mercy when the city was destroyed."

He picked up a small stone, turning it over in his hands. "The spies told her to tie a scarlet cord through her window. Everyone in her house would be spared."

Abner kept his gaze on the ruins. "And it worked?"

"It did," Eliab said. "The walls fell, but her household stood. You can still see it—that small section that did not crumble."

He traced a rough outline of a wall in the dust. "In that place, Rahab's house once stood."

Abner was silent for a moment.

The entire city had crumbled. But her house remained.

Just like his tree.

Eliab gestured toward the sycamore. "Like the trees that lose their leaves, the walls of Jericho were meant to fall. But just as your tree remains evergreen, God chose that one house to stand."

Something shifted in Abner's chest.

His tree was not weak because it remained unchanged—It was strong because God had made it so.

Just like Rahab's house.

Abner traced the young bark of his tree, thinking of Rahab. She had trusted the Lord when no one else did. She had welcomed the spies, protected them, and believed in the promise.

She had stood while all else fell.

"So... Rahab trusted, and God protected her," he said softly.

Eliab smiled. "Yes. And that is what faith does, my son. It doesn't promise ease. But when the seasons change, and everything else withers or falls, faith is what holds you upright."

Abner took a deep breath, his fingers brushing the leaves. For so long, he had worried about his tree. Now, for the first time, he realised his tree had always been strong.

And maybe, so was he.

That night, as Abner lay in bed, he listened to the wind moving through the trees. Some leaves danced away, rustling as they tumbled down the street.

But his tree?

It stood tall and full, whispering in the dark.

Before sleep came, Abner whispered into the quiet: "Stay strong, little tree."

And somewhere deep in his spirit, he heard the answer: *So will you.*

Chapter Ten:
A Shelter in the Wilderness

The streets of Jericho were alive with joy as the city prepared for Sukkot—the Feast of Tabernacles. All around, families were building sukkot, temporary booths and shelters made of wooden frames and shaded with palm fronds and leafy branches, shelters that would soon become the centre of celebration.

Children ran through the streets with willow and myrtle branches in their arms, their laughter ringing above the hum of voices. Merchants called from their stalls, offering baskets of figs, pomegranates, honey cakes, and dried dates. The warm air was filled with the mingling scents of baking bread, roasting lamb, and fresh fruit.

The city didn't just feel festive.

It felt alive.

Sukkot had always been a time of joy. But this year, for Abner, it meant something more.

Because this year... his tree had grown.

As he neared the courtyard, the sight caught him by surprise, though he had seen it every day.

There it stood—taller than him now, its branches wider, its leaves thick with colour, catching the sunlight as they swayed in the wind. The trunk had deepened in tone, firm beneath his hand. It wasn't fully grown, not yet. But it was strong. No longer something to be protected, but something beginning to offer protection.

Just like him.

He was no longer the boy who whispered over the soil. He had changed, too.

Up ahead, he saw his father.

Eliab carried wooden poles across his shoulder, his pace steady, though slower than it once had been. The lines in his face had deepened, and his steps bore the quiet rhythm of age.

"Abba! Let me help!" Abner called, jogging forward to relieve him of the palm branches bundled under his arm.

Eliab chuckled and exhaled slowly, shifting the weight. "Good. You're now strong enough to do more than carry the decorations." He smiled. "Thank God. I'm getting too old—and I certainly won't refuse help."

Hila walked beside them, a basket of ruby-red pomegranates in her arms, the juice staining her fingertips.

She was no longer a little girl hiding behind her mother's skirts. Her Bat Mitzvah had passed just months before. She moved with confidence now—eyes clear, shoulders lifted, her voice louder in family debates.

"I'm decorating the sukkah," she announced proudly. "Ima said I could."

Abner pulled her close for a moment, squeezing her tightly in a quick brotherly hug. "Then it'll be the most beautiful sukkah in all of Jericho."

She beamed and twirled away, her tunic flowing like a banner behind her as she ran inside to fetch garlands and fruit.

Together, father and son set to work.

They drove the wooden poles into the sunbaked earth, lashing them together with strips of cloth. They laid woven mats across the top and layered palm fronds thick enough for shade, but loose enough to let stars peek through.

When they were done, Abner stepped back and admired the work. "It's like a house."

Eliab nodded, wiping his brow. "Yes. But only for a short time."

Abner glanced upward at the open roof, where sky and branch interwove. "Why do we make it so flimsy?" he asked.

Eliab gestured to the booths now dotting rooftops and courtyards throughout the city.

"Because God commanded it," he said. "To remind us of the wilderness. When our people had no homes, only tents. No walls—only trust. That's why we sometimes call Him Adonai Machasenu."

Abner furrowed his brow. "The Lord is our Shelter?"

Eliab smiled. "Yes. We remember that He was our protection when we had nothing else."

Abner turned, his gaze falling upon his tree.

It had once been so small, helpless, barely a sprout. But now it stood tall, casting dappled shade onto the stones below.

He thought of his early fears. The storms. The doubts. The days when he'd whispered for it to grow.

It had endured.

Just as Israel had.

"But Abba," he said slowly, "we don't live in the wilderness anymore. We have homes. Walls. A city."

Eliab's hand rested on his shoulder.

"Exactly. And that is why we build these shelters."

Abner looked up at him, waiting.

"To remind us," Eliab said. "To remember where we came from. To never forget that even now, with walls and houses and comfort, we still depend on God."

He pointed toward the tree.

"Look at it. Strong, isn't it?"

Abner nodded with pride. "Very."

"But do you remember how small it was?" Eliab asked. "How you worried for it? How you protected it?"

Abner could still feel it—his fingers scraping at the soil, the lump in his throat when it nearly died, the thrill when the first leaf appeared.

"I remember."

Eliab knelt beside the tree and placed his hand gently on the bark.

"This," he said, "is Sukkot. This is why we build temporary shelters. Because once we, too, were vulnerable. And God gave us the strength to grow."

Abner looked again at the tree.

It had not grown on its own.

It had been watered.

Guarded.

Remembered.

And blessed.

As twilight settled over Jericho, their family gathered in the sukkah, the roof now blanketed in palm and fig leaves, grapes hanging in garlands above. The warm light of oil lamps flickered, casting soft shadows across the woven walls. The scent of roasted vegetables and cinnamon bread filled the space. Bowls of figs, dates, and olives lay between plates of honey-glazed lamb and flatbread.

Naamah set down a dish of sweet cakes and smiled as she took her seat beside Eliab.

"The best part of Sukkot," she said, "is sharing with those you love."

Hila nodded, plucking a fig from the bowl. "And eating."

Abner laughed, lifting his cup of pomegranate juice in agreement.

Eliab raised his hands and began the blessing, his voice deep and full of quiet joy:

"Baruch atah Adonai, Eloheinu Melech ha'olam, Shehechiyanu, v'kiy'manu, v'higiyanu lazman hazeh…"

Blessed are You, Lord our God, King of the universe, who has given us life, sustained us, and enabled us to reach this season.

Then, he took up the lulav—the palm branch bundled with willow and myrtle—and the etrog, the citron fruit. He waved them in every direction—north, south, east, and west—then up and down, a declaration that God's presence fills the earth.

Abner watched the leaves shimmer as the lulav moved. His heart stirred.

His tree had once needed him.

Now it stood on its own.

But its strength had come from something more than water or sun.

It had come from above.

As the family ate, laughed, and sang, Abner slipped out from the sukkah and sat beneath the tree. Its leaves swayed gently above him, catching the night breeze. Stars blinked into view overhead, scattered like grain upon black soil.

He leaned back against the trunk.

It was solid.

Warm.

Alive.

He closed his eyes and listened—the soft rustling of leaves, his father's voice singing from the sukkah, the faint jingle of a goat's bell

| *Planted for a purpose*

in the distance.

And somewhere in the quiet, he heard it again.

That whisper.

The tree is growing.

He opened his eyes and looked upward through the branches.

Did it have a purpose?

Would someone climb it one day?

Would it give fruit?

Would it shelter another child, long after he was gone?

He didn't know.

Not yet.

But one day, he would.

And perhaps, just perhaps… the tree already knew.

Chapter Eleven:
First Fruits

The morning sun was warm on Abner's face as he stepped into the courtyard, stretching the sleep from his limbs like a cloak shaken out after rest. His tunic clung lightly to his back, still damp from the night's lingering cool, and he blinked against the amber light that gilded the stone walls in gold.

The air was rich with the scent of softened earth, the ground still yielding beneath his sandals from the evening's rain. From beyond the courtyard wall, the low murmur of the waking marketplace drifted toward him—wooden carts creaking, donkeys braying, and the sing-song calls of vendors arranging their wares. A breeze stirred, carrying the sweet perfume of ripening fruit—figs, pomegranates, and citrus—intertwined with the earthy aroma of dust, dew, and crushed leaves.

But something was different this morning.

He couldn't explain it—not in words. It wasn't the weather, or the sounds, or even the scent in the air. It was something deeper. A stillness beneath the stir. A hush within the hum. A pause in the rhythm of all that was familiar.

He felt it before he saw it.

His gaze turned instinctively, as it always did, to the far side of the courtyard—toward the sycamore fig tree. No longer a fragile sapling, it stood tall now, anchored and assured. The trunk had thickened into strength, and its canopy of leaves shimmered in the morning light,

Planted for a purpose

rustling softly like whispered prayers.

Abner's heart skipped.

He stepped closer—slowly, deliberately—as if approaching something sacred. And then he saw it.

Nestled among the folds of the green leaves, half-sheltered in shadow, half-bathed in gold—

A fig.

His fig.

The first fruit.

He drew a breath, deep and unsteady, wonder swelling in his chest like a psalm rising—wordless but full.

For a moment, he just stared. In wondrous awe.

Then his body surged forward, and his hand parted the leaves to see more clearly. It was small—barely the size of a closed fist—and still tinged with green at the edges. But it was whole. Real. A promise, finally fulfilled.

His heart thudded against his ribs like the pounding of a distant drum. "A fruit!" he breathed, the words slipping out half-laugh, half-gasp. His knees felt strangely weak.

Years. Years of waiting, of watering in silence, shielding it from storms and the scorching summer heat. Years of chasing off goats and reckless boys. Of clearing weeds, watching, and hoping. He had whispered to the tree when no one else was listening, urging it to hold on, to grow, to live.

And now... it had listened. It had answered.

A grin spread across his face, slow and wide. Not just pride—it was something deeper. Wonder. Gratitude. Fulfilment.

He had imagined this day so many times. But standing here now, the moment felt more sacred than he'd ever pictured—too holy to rush, too real to believe.

"Abba!" he called, his voice cracking under the weight of joy. "Come quickly!"

From within the house came the rustling of fabric and the soft scuff of sandals against stone. Eliab emerged into the courtyard, blinking at the brightness, wiping his hands on a worn linen cloth. His beard now bore silver rather than black, and though his steps were much slower, there was a strength in him still—rooted, enduring. Like the very tree his son had tended all these years.

"What is it, my son?" Eliab asked, his voice roughened with age, yet carrying that familiar thread of warmth and affection.

Abner could hardly contain himself. He pointed toward the tree, words tumbling over each other. "Look!"

Eliab followed the direction of his son's arm, and when his eyes settled on the fig, his face softened into a quiet smile. He didn't rush. Instead, he stood still, letting the moment breathe, allowing its beauty to settle upon him like morning dew.

Then, with the slow certainty of age, he walked the worn pathway to the tree. Each step deliberate. Each breath, perhaps, a silent prayer of thanks. Reaching the tree, he laid his hand gently on the bark, as though greeting an old friend. His fingers lingered there, reverent.

"It has begun," he said softly, his eyes turning to Abner. "Your tree has answered the seasons."

Abner nodded, heart pounding with joy and disbelief, his body restless with the thrill of fulfilment. "I've waited so long, Abba! Can I pick it? Just this one?"

Eliab's expression shifted—something reflective flickered behind his eyes. "Do you remember what the Torah commands about the first fruits?"

Planted for a purpose

The question landed like a pebble dropped into still water, sending quiet ripples through Abner's heart. His smile faltered.

He searched his father's face, the words coming slowly, drawn from memory—Shabbat lessons, the rhythm of ancient teachings, Eliab's voice echoing from evenings past. "Remember, the first belongs to the Lord," he said at last, the truth settling heavy in his mouth.

Eliab nodded, calm and unwavering. "Yes. Before we take for ourselves, we give to Him."

Abner glanced down at the fruit cradled in his hand. It looked so simple, unassuming in its form. Yet to him, it was everything. To give it before tasting it... felt like surrendering a piece of himself.

"But I've waited so long, Abba," he murmured, protest tinging the edges of his voice.

Eliab placed a steady hand on his son's shoulder. "And that is precisely why it must be given."

Abner looked up, the lines in his face firmer now, the boyishness faded into something older, more questioning. His brow furrowed. His heart warred with obedience.

"When something costs you nothing," Eliab continued, his tone soft but resolute, "it is easy to offer. But this fruit, this first fruit, is sacred because it means so much to you. You tended this tree as a shepherd guards his flock. You wept when it wilted. You sang to it in solitude. You protected it from wind, and heat, and doubt. And now, its promise has come. But before you enjoy the blessing, you must remember the Giver."

Abner swallowed, the lump in his throat forming like stone. He understood. He didn't want to—but he did.

And then came a voice, jarring and familiar—like thorns dragging through cloth.

"Still fussing over that tree, Abner?"

He turned sharply, jaw tightening.

Barak.

Standing at the entrance of the courtyard, arms folded and eyes scanning the scene, Barak appeared older, broader through the shoulders, skin darkened by sun and distance. Dust clung thick to his sandals, and a traveller's bag rested across one shoulder, worn from use. Yet the expression on his face—half sneer, half challenge—had not changed since they were boys.

Memories rose unbidden: Barak's heel crushing the fragile sapling. The scuffle in the dirt. The sting of fists. The ache of bruised pride and the deeper wound of shame.

Abner drew himself upright, shoulders squared, voice level. "It's not just any tree, Barak."

Barak scoffed. "Looks like a tree to me." His tone curled with derision.

The air tensed—but Eliab's voice cut through it, warm and steady, yet unyielding. "Come closer, Barak."

Barak's eyes narrowed. Suspicion flickered. "Why?"

"Because there's something you need to see."

With apparent reluctance, Barak stepped into the courtyard. His sandals scuffed the earth as he moved, leaving careless tracks in the soil Abner had once guarded so fiercely. He gave the tree a passing glance, unmoved.

"This," Eliab said, motioning toward the fruit still resting in Abner's careful grasp, "is its first fruit."

Barak squinted, unmoved. "So?"

Eliab didn't answer immediately. He crouched—his joints slow, deliberate—and reached for the small wicker basket resting beside

| *Planted for a purpose*

the tree. With quiet ceremony, he set it down between the two young men.

A silent offering.

A line drawn.

An invitation—and a reckoning.

"Do you know why we give the first to the Lord?"

Barak rolled his eyes. "Of course. It's the law. The first of the harvest goes to God."

"And why is that?" Eliab asked, his voice gentle but insistent.

Barak shifted his weight, looking away with a shrug. "Because... we trust there'll be more."

Eliab's eyes twinkled—that knowing gleam Abner recognised well. The kind that carried more than words. "So, you do understand, Barak."

Barak frowned, folding his arms tighter across his chest. Abner, standing a little taller beside his father, allowed himself a faint, almost reluctant smile. There was no triumph in it—only recognition.

Eliab straightened, his hand brushing the bark of the tree as though reading its rings with his fingertips. "When our people wandered the wilderness, we had no land. No fields. No trees. Nothing to call our own. And yet, we lacked nothing. God fed us with manna. Drew water from a rock. Sent quail when we grumbled that there was meat in Egypt but none in the desert. We learned—sometimes the hard way— not to trust in what we held... but in Who held us."

He took the fig from Abner's hand, holding it up where the sunlight struck it. Its skin shimmered with a sheen of promise.

"Now we have land. We have trees that bear fruit. But before we taste, we remember—" his voice softened, reverent, "—it is not the fruit that sustains us, but the One who makes it grow."

Barak's gaze lingered on the fig. Something in his stance shifted—

not much, but enough. The set of his jaw loosened. His arms fell slightly from their folded defence. A flicker crossed his face—quiet, unreadable.

But it was something.

Eliab continued, his voice quieter now. "If we do not give, we forget. And forgetting leads to pride. And pride... that leads to ruin."

Barak said nothing.

"Do you remember Cain and Abel?" Eliab asked the boys gently.

Barak nodded. "Cain offered crops. Abel offered a lamb."

"Yes. And God accepted only one. Do you know why?"

Barak hesitated. Abner answered instead. "Because Abel gave in faith. And Cain didn't."

Eliab smiled faintly. "Yes. Cain gave what was convenient. Abel gave what was costly. And God saw the heart behind the gift."

A hush settled over them, like a soft wind brushing through the leaves.

Barak looked at the fig again. This time, he didn't scoff.

Eliab handed it back to Abner. "Take it to the synagogue, my son. Offer it in thanksgiving to God. And then—wait. Wait in faith. For there will be more."

Abner nodded. This time, there was no hesitation.

He turned to go.

Then, pausing beside Barak, he asked quietly, "Would you like to come?"

Barak blinked, caught off guard. His mouth opened, but no words came.

And then—after a long pause—he nodded.

"...Alright."

Eliab smiled to himself, leaning against the tree as his son and

Planted for a purpose

Barak walked into the morning light, their shadows long behind them, their voices low and steady. Two former rivals, now side by side. Brought together by a tree planted in faith and words of trust from the scriptures.

"He'll be alright," Eliab whispered to himself, as if speaking into his spirit. "As God has taught you to grow, He is teaching my son, one lesson at a time."

He placed his hand gently upon the bark, steadying himself, then looked to the heavens with quiet eyes.

"O Lord, God of our fathers... let him walk before You in truth, with all his heart and with all his soul. And may this house—this life— be planted firm."

Behind Abner and Barak, the breeze stirred through the branches of the fig tree—a whisper of promise—a sigh of something new.

The tree stood tall in the courtyard, bearing witness—a standard of faith.

And the first fruit they carried to offer was only the beginning.

Chapter Twelve:
The Weight of Inheritance

The afternoon sun filtered through the branches of Abner's tree, casting dappled shadows that danced across the smooth stones of the courtyard. Light shifted gently with the breeze—the same breeze that stirred the leaves above like whispers from another time. The tree, once a trembling sprout barely clinging to life in the hard-packed soil, now stood resolute—its trunk thick and weathered, its roots hidden but deep, unshaken.

Abner stood beneath it, his hand resting on the bark as though drawing strength from the very fibres of the tree itself. His fingers traced its grain slowly, reverently—the way one might trace the carved letters of a headstone. There was a silence in the courtyard. Not the absence of sound, but a sacred stillness. The kind that comes when something permanent has left the world.

He had stood here so many times before—seeking answers, comfort, perspective.

But today, the ground felt different beneath his feet. Uneven. Uncertain. He could not name it at first. But it was not the soil that had shifted.

It was himself.

It had been a week since his father was gone.

The finality of it caught him off guard. Even after the prayers, the mourning, the gathering of neighbours who spoke of Eliab's wisdom and strength, still, a part of Abner had expected to hear that familiar voice once more and expected to turn and find his father behind him, arms folded, eyes amused but knowing.

But now... there would be no more questions answered.

No more gentle corrections.

No more warm, calloused hands resting on his shoulder when words failed.

The absence pressed in like a weight on his chest—heavy, unfamiliar, unyielding.

He had not known until now how much of himself had leaned on the strength of that man—his abba.

A soft rustling of fabric behind him stirred the stillness, and he turned, startled.

Naamah stood in the archway, the fading sunlight softening the creases that grief had etched more deeply into her face. Her once-dark hair was now streaked with silver, pulled back in a loose braid. Her steps were slower, her hands trembled slightly—but her posture remained regal. There was grace in her bearing, a quiet endurance that sorrow had not managed to break.

Without a word, she crossed the courtyard and lowered herself onto the stone bench beneath the tree—the bench where Eliab had often sat in the hush of evening. Her hands smoothed the fabric of her robe with absent-minded care. Then she looked up at her son and offered him a smile that didn't quite reach her eyes.

"You look so much like your father when you stand there, Abner," she said at last, her voice gentle but edged with the ache of memory. "The way you tilt your head. The way you touch the tree. It's as if I'm looking at him again."

Abner blinked hard, his throat tightening. He didn't want to speak, but the words came anyway.

"I don't feel like him, Ima."

He looked away, his voice quiet, breaking. "How am I supposed to do this?"

Naamah's gaze lifted to the swaying branches overhead. "Neither did Joshua... when Moses was gone."

Abner turned to her, puzzled by the sudden turn toward Scripture. "Ima?"

"Your Abba often spoke of that moment," she said softly. "He always admired how Joshua stepped forward—not because he was ready, but because he was obedient. Moses was gone. The one who led them out of Egypt, through the wilderness, who spoke with God face to face... was gone. And the weight fell on Joshua. Alone."

She paused, her voice thickening with emotion. "But then the Lord spoke to him: *'Be strong and courageous. Do not be afraid or discouraged, for the Lord your God is with you wherever you go.'*"

The words landed differently today. Abner had heard them countless times growing up—quoted in Shabbat lessons, echoed in his father's voice beside the evening fire—but now they fell like rain on dry ground, soaking into places he hadn't known were parched.

Naamah turned her gaze fully to him. "Abner, a leader is not measured by how ready he feels. He is measured by whether he trusts that God is still leading, especially when he no longer hears a voice beside him."

Abner said nothing. His fingers curled tightly against the bark. He hated this feeling—this hollow ache of uncertainty. Of being small.

"But Abba..." he murmured. "He always knew what to say."

A faint smile touched Naamah's lips. "Because he had many years to learn how to listen. And from listening, he learned."

She gave a soft, breathy laugh. "When your father was young, he didn't always get it right. He stumbled. He questioned. He even resisted. But he never stopped listening. And when he listened, he knew."

Her hand reached out and gently touched his wrist—brief, steady.

"And now, my son… it is your turn to listen. To wait and to trust in your listening."

A breeze passed between them, calm and quiet. Dust swirled lazily near their feet, as though even the earth paused to consider her words. Abner looked down at the smooth, worn stones—how many times had Eliab stood here? Teaching. Correcting. Laughing. Praying.

Now those footprints were fading.

And there was no one left to stand in that place.

No one… except him.

He was no longer the boy full of questions.

He was the one meant to carry the answers.

A soft rustling from the entryway drew his gaze.

Hila.

She stepped lightly into the courtyard, her blue dress catching the sunlight as it fluttered around her ankles. In her arms was a woven basket filled with deep red pomegranates, their skins glistening with a rich, deep red hue. She had grown into her womanhood quietly, steadily—like the tree behind him. She was no longer the girl who ran barefoot through the fields trailing after him. Her face was composed, her bearing graceful.

Abner felt a tug in his heart—a bittersweet recognition. Time had moved on, even when he hadn't noticed.

"You've been out here a while, Abner," she said, her voice soft but sure.

He nodded. "Just thinking."

She stepped forward and took his hand in hers, grounding him. Her touch reminded him of when they were children, clinging to each other in fear or joy. Now, it steadied him once again.

"I miss him too," she said quietly, and those simple words broke something loose in his chest.

He looked away. "But how do we go on without him, Hila? How do I?"

She was quiet for a moment. Then, with a gentle firmness, she replied, "We go on the same way he taught us to live—by trusting the One who sees further than we do. This is God's will, and we continue to walk in it. He has been faithful, and He will continue to be so."

Abner exhaled slowly. "I know. But everything feels... weightier now. Like I'm meant to hold it all together, and I'm not sure I know how."

"You're not meant to hold it all," she said, releasing his hand. "Just what has been entrusted to you."

He gave a tired laugh, but there was no humour in it. "That's the part I don't know—the role that has been entrusted to me. What if I fail?"

"You won't."

"You don't know that."

She moved toward the base of the tree and set down the basket, then turned and leaned against the trunk, mirroring his posture. "I see it, you know," she added, her gaze steady. "The way you carry yourself now. It's different. There's strength in it. Even when you don't feel it."

Abner shook his head slightly. "I don't feel it though, Hila, but I should. I want to still hear his voice in the quiet, telling me what to do. I think I'll always want to ask him first."

"That's not weakness," she said. "That's honour. You show honour to our abba that way. And wisdom."

He turned his face away, blinking back the rising sting in his eyes. "I just keep thinking… maybe if I listen hard enough, I'll still hear him."

Her expression softened, her voice like a thread woven with memory. "Then listen, Abner. Listen with everything in you. Because the words he spoke over you… they were born of his faith in God. Just like the scriptures and the promises—they echo, long after the voice itself is gone."

He glanced at her, eyes searching. "You sound like him now."

She smiled faintly. "So do you. We all carry a part of him. You… you carry the part that leads."

"And clearly, you, the wisdom," Abner replied, the faintest of smiles breaking through his troubled countenance.

A silence settled between them, comfortable, knowing.

Then Hila spoke again, more cautiously this time. "I was speaking with Ima earlier."

Abner raised an eyebrow. "Oh?"

"There was talk," she said slowly, "of the future."

A pause.

"She mentioned… betrothal."

The word lingered in the air, delicate as spun glass.

He blinked. "Betrothal?"

Hila nodded. "Yes. There are a few families. One in particular."

Hila didn't elaborate. She didn't need to. Abner felt a strange swell in his chest—something between pride, sorrow, and quiet displacement—his little sister, soon to be someone's wife.

Life was already shifting again. Without pause. Without permission.

He found himself wishing it would slow, just for a while. Just long enough to breathe. But even in loss, he knew—life keeps on going... and growing.

"Are you ready for that?" he asked softly, not quite trusting his voice.

"I think so," she said, considering his question. Then she hesitated. Her smile was small, but it reached her eyes. "I think I'm beginning to be."

Abner nodded, though his chest tightened. Their family was changing. The circle that had once felt unbreakable was now thinning, reshaping. There was grief in it—but growth, too. People stepping forward. Others stepping away. Into new paths, new places.

He could not hold it all still. Nor should he. Perhaps this was a natural part of life, a part and sign of maturity.

Naamah was still sitting on the stone bench beneath the tree, silently watching them deep in conversation hadn't spoken until now, but her voice, when it came, was calm and sure, carrying the quiet wisdom that always seemed to come from her.

"Time does not wait for us, my son. It moves forward whether we are ready or not. That is a lesson we all must learn, with every turning of life."

Abner looked from his sister to his mother, then back to the tree—always, the tree.

He placed his hand against the trunk. Somehow, this place grounded him. The tree stood firm now in storms, in sorrow, in sun. His palm ran along the bark, and for the first time in days, he felt something shift within him.

Not peace. Not certainty.

But strength.

The kind that rises not when you feel ready, but when you know the next step must still be taken.

"How many times," he whispered to himself, "have I come here seeking answers?"

No one responded. But he didn't need them to. The answers were already planted. Not given, but grown. And now, he was the one meant to tend them. He turned back to the women who stood at the heart of his family, and knew—this was his season to lead.

They were in their own seasons too. Naamah, in the twilight of wisdom. Hila, standing at the threshold of new beginnings. But for him, this was the hour to step into leading the family.

"Then it's time we step forward too," he said firmly. "Together. As a family."

Naamah's lips curved into a smile that held both blessing and release.

Hila stepped forward and embraced him. Her arms around him felt like memory and promise all at once—an anchor, and a farewell.

The wind stirred the branches above, and Abner breathed in deeply. He would carry his father's lessons with him. He would carry the weight. And he would stand—like Joshua once stood. Like his tree still stood.

For the first time since Eliab's death, he knew he would not fall.

A quiet prayer rose in his heart.

Not shouted. Not spoken aloud.

But received.

"Adonai... I do not have the answers.

Nor the strength.

But give me ears to hear, and a heart to obey.

Teach me to lead as one who follows You first."

He was no longer the boy who asked, he was the man who would carry.

And he trusted the One who gives.

Chapter Thirteen:
A Celebration Beneath the Tree

She stood with her hands clasped gently before her, her dress of soft ivory brushing the tops of her sandals, stitched with threads the colour of sunrise. Her hair, braided with delicate ribbons and tucked with tiny white blossoms, caught the last golden light as though heaven itself had touched her brow.

All eyes were drawn to her, not only for her beauty, but for the quiet confidence she carried. The young girl who once ran barefoot through the fields had become a woman whose strength came not from volume, but from stillness.

Abner stood near the entrance; his breath caught somewhere between awe and memory. This moment—this evening—felt more like a page from Scripture than a scene from ordinary life.

He could almost hear Eliab's voice: *"A time to plant, and a time to reap. A time to be born... and a time to build."*

Spring had ushered in its fullness, not just in the buds and fruit of the land, but in the turning of seasons within their family.

And this evening—*this* evening—was a third day.

Not by mere calendar, but by blessing.

For it was on the third day of Creation that God had spoken twice: "It was good... it was good."

And so, without needing to explain it aloud, Abner knew what his mother had meant when she'd whispered earlier, *"Today is a good day, my son. A double portion kind of day."*

The music began to rise—slow, steady, ancient.

Abner stepped forward to escort his sister beneath the canopy.

As he did, the fig tree swayed gently in the evening breeze.

It had not been dressed for the occasion. No ribbons, no oil lamps. And yet—it stood tall, noble, alive.

Bearing witness.

Just as it always had.

As Abner reached her side, Hila turned slightly, and their eyes met.

No words were spoken, but something passed between them—unspoken understanding, shared history, silent blessing.

She gave the faintest nod, not for permission, but for peace.

Abner extended his arm. She placed her hand upon it, her fingers warm and steady. He could feel her pulse beneath the silk, sure and calm, like the rhythm of a psalm well remembered.

The music shifted, the flute and lyre weaving together a melody both joyful and ancient, the rhythm of a wedding long foretold. A hand-drum pulsed softly beneath it, steady as a heartbeat, echoing through the gathering hush. And together, they stepped forward.

Past the rows of gathered guests, faces both familiar and distant, lit by lamp and starlight. Past Naamah, who stood with hands folded at her breast, her eyes full of tears and pride. Past neighbours who had watched them grow, who had once whispered prayers over their cradle-songs and their scraped knees.

The path beneath their feet was strewn with olive branches and petals. A symbol of peace. A sign of blessing.

And the chuppah waited—white linen gently stirring like a sigh in the still air.

It wasn't just a shelter. It was a signpost.

Of covenant. Of covering. Of sacred beginnings.

As they reached its edge, Abner paused and looked at his sister one last time before releasing her hand.

He didn't speak. He didn't need to.

Instead, he bowed his head, offering not just a farewell, but a prayer.

A blessing for the journey ahead.

Then, with hands now empty but heart full, he stepped back.

And Hila stepped forward.

Into promise. Into joy. Into the life that was now hers to build.

And above them, the sky deepened—stars emerging like whispered amens.

Abner caught her gaze and saw it—hidden behind her composure, the faint tremble of her fingers, the unshed tears shimmering in the corners of her eyes. She stood still, hands clasped gently in front of her, but the rise and fall of her chest told him all he needed to know. Her breath was steady, but fragile, like the hush before a sacred vow.

He reached her and gently took her hand.

His fingers brushed the embroidery on her sleeve, and a hundred memories flooded his mind—of her small hand gripping his tunic, of laughter under fig trees, of her curls tangled in the wind. He remembered her sitting beside him on dusty stone steps, legs swinging as she peppered him with questions about God and the world. And now... he would place that same precious hand into another's.

He turned his head slightly, glancing toward the sycamore tree just beyond the gathering. Its massive trunk stood like a guardian, its branches wide and embracing, its leaves whispering in the breeze. How many hours had he spent beneath it? How many lessons had he heard spoken under its shade? How many silent prayers had risen from its roots to the heavens? And now, tonight, it stood watch again—this time, over a new chapter.

He imagined his father there.

Eliab would have stood with him. Would have clasped his shoulder. Would have kissed Hila's forehead and whispered something wise. Something only a father could say. Something that settled a soul.

But even in the absence, Abner felt his father's nearness. The sycamore bore silent witness. It had stood through seasons of drought and rain, of joy and mourning. Tonight, it stood still and sure, like Eliab once had.

As he placed Hila's hand into her groom's, a quiet strength rose within him. He lifted his chin, meeting his sister's eyes.

She smiled through tears. Not of sadness, but of fullness. The kind of fullness that only comes when love and grief share the same breath.

In that moment, everything stilled.

And then he spoke the ancient words, passing her hand into the keeping of her new family.

The rabbi began to chant the blessings over the ketubah, the marriage contract, his voice rich and melodic, echoing over the gathered assembly. The rhythm of Hebrew verse wrapped around them like a prayer, binding hearts, homes, and futures in covenant. Each syllable, ancient and enduring, seemed to settle into the stones beneath their feet, as though even the earth recognised the holiness of the moment.

Naamah sat near the front, veiled and robed in ceremonial white. Her silver hair peeked through beneath the delicate cloth, and though her frame was more petite and frailer now, there was a quiet majesty in her posture. Her spine straight, her chin slightly lifted, she looked every bit the matriarch she had become. Her eyes shimmered as they took in the sight—her daughter beneath the chuppah, her son beside her, fulfilling the role Eliab once would have taken. Her hands, worn from years of labour and love, were folded softly in her lap, fingers gently intertwined.

Abner caught her gaze, wondering what memories were stirring behind those wise eyes. Perhaps she was hearing her own wedding songs again—melodies carried on desert wind, wrapped in laughter and young hope.

Perhaps she was seeing Eliab's smile in Hila's—echoes of the man who once held her hand under the same stars.

A breeze passed through the courtyard, lifting the linen canopy, stirring the olive branches overhead. The ribbons danced again, as if Heaven itself were rejoicing. Their movement was not wild, but reverent—like a chorus swaying in time with the blessing.

Abner inhaled deeply.

The tree had grown as they had grown. No longer a sapling in uncertain soil, it now stood resolute—a witness to grief, to growth, to grace.

And now, as its branches reached toward the stars, so too did Hila reach toward her new life.

When the moment came, he lifted her palm once more, this time with finality. He paused—not from hesitation, but from reverence. The air seemed to still with him, as if the heavens were waiting too.

Her eyes met his again.

And in them, he saw love.

Not the playful love of a sister for her older brother, but the deep, thankful love of one who knew she had been protected, guided, cherished. A love that understood the cost of care. A love that honoured the years between them.

He smiled. And the weight lifted.

She would be alright.

She would be loved.

He let go.

And in that letting go, something sacred passed between them—unspoken, eternal.

The courtyard erupted in jubilant celebration.

Laughter rang out as music soared—stringed instruments, tambourines, and the rhythm of hands clapping joyously in time. The men danced jubilantly, stamping feet and raising voices in ancient melodies. The women swirled in a cascade of colour, sleeves flowing, braids swinging, laughter echoing into the night. Plates were passed, laden with roasted lamb, dates soaked in honey, warm flatbread, and sweet cakes dusted with almond and cinnamon.

Wine flowed from clay jugs, poured freely—a sign of blessing and abundance, the master of ceremonies watching to ensure all was in order: that no cup sat empty, no guest went unnoticed, no serving table lacked bread or fruit. He moved quietly among the servants, offering brief nods and murmured instructions, attentive to every detail yet never drawing attention to himself.

Near the edge of the gathering, beneath the glow of lanterns strung between fig and palm, Naamah sat and watched. Her eyes brimmed with unshed tears—not from grief, but from that sacred ache only a mother knows. She would often say, "I'm not losing a daughter, but rather gaining another son," and she meant it. But the truth lingered quietly beneath the words—her daughter would be leaving the family home. The rhythms of daily life would change. The familiar footsteps, the laughter echoing from the courtyard, the shared moments between mother and daughter—these would now belong to another household. And though her heart rejoiced, it ached too.

Hila appeared by her side, slipping momentarily away from the dancers. She knelt, careful not to wrinkle her robes, and took Naamah's hands in her own.

Leaning forward, "Ima," she said softly, "are you well?"

Naamah reached out and gently tucked a loose curl behind her daughter's ear, her touch lingering with quiet affection. "Better than well, child. You are a bride today. And such a beautiful one."

Her voice caught slightly, and her hands trembled with tenderness as they settled over Hila's. "I always knew this day would come," she whispered. "But I did not know it would come so quickly."

She paused, eyes glistening. "You were just a child—barefoot in the courtyard, asking endless questions, singing when you thought no one was listening."

She exhaled shakily. "Your Abba... he would have wept with pride. He would have taken your hand himself and kissed your brow."

Hila leaned forward, resting her forehead against her mother's. "It is because of you, Ima, that I am ready for this day…"

She paused, then added, her voice hushed but sure, "…and for all the days to come."

Naamah closed her eyes at the words, and for a moment, mother and daughter simply breathed—two hearts, bound by love, memory, and faith in what lay ahead.

Naamah chuckled lightly. "Every bride says that. Until she is washing dishes and chasing children and wondering how she'll get it all done before sunset."

They both laughed softly.

Then Naamah drew her close. "But never forget. You will always have a place here."

"And I will always return."

A shadow crossed the stones.

Abner.

He knelt beside both of them, his presence warm and solid. One hand came to rest on his mother's shoulder; the other reached for Hila's.

"Are you happy, little sister?"

She smirked through her tears. "Will you call me that forever?"

"Yes," he replied with a grin. "Even when you're old and grey."

Then his smile softened into something gentler.

"Truly, Hila... are you happy?"

She nodded, her lips parting in a breathless smile.

"Yes, Abner. I am. More than I ever imagined I would be."

He lingered, watching her, holding this moment like a photograph in his heart. Then he leaned forward and kissed her brow.

"Then I am happy too."

Naamah's eyes twinkled. "It is your turn next, my son."

Abner threw his head back and laughed. "Ima, please... let me dance before you start choosing my bride."

Naamah raised an eyebrow. "We shall see."

The music swelled again. Hila rose, kissed her mother once more, and rejoined the circle of dancers, her laughter rising like incense into the stars.

Abner remained, watching, letting the music wash over him. Letting the moment settle.

Naamah gave his hand a light squeeze, then released it without a word, as if sensing he needed space. He stood slowly, his gaze trailing after his sister, then drifting toward the edge of the courtyard.

Without thinking, his feet carried him to the place he always returned to.

The sycamore tree. His tree.

Its branches swayed gently above, rustling like a lullaby only the night could hear. He placed a hand against the bark—rough, familiar, grounding. The glow of nearby lanterns danced across the trunk, casting shifting patterns at his feet.

Here, the world quieted.

Then—

A voice, soft as the wind, broke into his thoughts.

"You look deep in thought."

He turned.

A young woman stood nearby, just beyond the circle of lantern light, yet somehow still illuminated by firelight, by starlight, perhaps by something more. Her hair, dark and wind-tossed, fell in loose waves around her face, framing features both gentle and quietly resolute. There was no ornament in her hair, no fine jewellery or silken trim—only the simplicity of presence. And still, she drew his eyes.

Her robe was woven from pale flax, unassuming yet elegant, with blue embroidery stitched along the sleeves—simple vines and tiny flowers, catching the light like whispers of water in moonlight. She stood with the ease of someone who did not need attention to feel secure in her place.

Abner recognised her vaguely. Perhaps the daughter of a family from the next village over—one of the invited households. But there was something about her that felt... familiar, though he could not place why.

Her eyes were deep and clear, like wells that held more than surface reflection.

He nodded, slightly guarded. "I suppose I am."

"She is your sister?" the woman asked, stepping a little closer, her voice low and melodic.

"Yes," he replied.

"She looks very happy."

His gaze shifted across the courtyard to where Hila danced again—radiant, laughing, twirling between friends and new family.

"She always has been," he said, a trace of wonder in his tone, as if noticing it anew.

A moment passed between them. Not an awkward pause, but a shared quiet, like standing beside someone watching the same sunset.

Then her eyes moved to the tree.

"This tree... it is yours?" she asked.

He blinked, caught off guard. "Yes. How did you know?"

Her lips curved slightly, a knowing smile forming—unhurried, almost amused.

"Because of the way you look at it," she said softly. "The same way you looked at your sister. As if it holds something sacred... something set apart. A meaning deeper than most would usually see."

She took a slow step forward and extended her hand, fingertips brushing the bark as though she, too, recognised something living in it. "It's beautiful," she murmured, more to the tree than to him.

Abner swallowed.

"Yes," he said softly.

But he wasn't looking at the tree anymore.

She turned toward him fully now, stepping into the halo of lantern light.

"What is your name?" he asked, his voice lower than before—part wonder, part prayer.

Her lips curved into a smile, soft and unhurried, as if she'd known he would ask.

"Rachel," she said.

He let the name settle in his mind.

Rachel.

It lingered there like a psalm—simple, sacred, familiar in a way that defied explanation. The name of the one Jacob had chosen. The one he worked willingly for fourteen years to marry. The favoured wife, the beloved. Her name carried the echo of devotion, of patient pursuit, of love that waited and did not waver.

And though the music played on—though laughter echoed, feet stamped, and joy swirled in vibrant waves around them—Abner found himself glancing across the courtyard again and again.

Drawn.

Intrigued.

Something in him stirred—like a memory not yet lived—each time her eyes found his.

And each time, her smile met his like a promise unspoken—but deeply understood.

Not rushed.

Not forced.

But planted.

And like Abner's seed from his childhood, it began to grow.

Chapter Fourteen:
Emunah

The laughter of children rang through the air long before Abner even saw them. He straightened, wiping his hands on his tunic, bracing himself for the coming storm—a flurry of little feet, eager voices, and arms that would soon be wrapped ever so tightly around him and unwilling to set him free.

A cloud of dust rose in the distance, kicked up by the small running feet of Hila's children down the road. Their voices carried over the warm breeze, full of excitement and joy as they raced toward the courtyard, eager for time with their dod and doda. The olive trees swayed gently above them, as if bowing in welcome. Behind them, Hila and her husband followed at a steady pace, baskets wrapped in cloth balanced in their arms, the tell-tale scent of warm dates and flatbread wafting ahead of them like a gentle herald.

They were coming.

Abner smiled. He always felt this way when his sister and her family visited—like a familiar song returning, a melody of laughter, love, and memories. Hila hadn't changed much over the years, though the gentle touch of motherhood had softened her features and brought a new depth to her eyes. She walked with the quiet grace of a woman who had learned much, endured much, and carried it all with wisdom.

Planted for a purpose

Rachel stepped out from the house, brushing flour from her hands onto her apron. The sunlight caught in the delicate strands of her hair, and the scent of yeast and honey clung to her like a second garment. The moment she caught sight of them, her face lit up—that same beautiful smile Abner remembered from the night they first met at Hila's wedding. It had not faded with time.

"They're here," she said softly, the warmth in her voice unmistakable.

Abner nodded just as the first of the children barrelled into him, a blur of laughter and small limbs. Tiny arms wrapped around his waist with surprising force, squeals of "Dod Abner! Dod Abner!" filling the air as giggles bubbled up, and he stumbled back slightly, nearly losing his footing on the packed earth.

"You've grown since I last saw you," he chuckled, ruffling the boy's dark curls, which bounced with the motion. "What are they feeding you—mountain lion meat?"

The children erupted into laughter at Abner's comment. He always seemed to know just what to say—and how to say it—to warm their hearts. One of them grinned proudly, puffing out his chest, while another clung tightly to Abner's leg, refusing to let go.

Hila laughed as she approached, shifting the weight of the basket in her arms. "That's what happens when time keeps moving, brother. Something I'm sure you've noticed."

Abner exhaled, shaking his head with amusement. "Yes. I've noticed," he said, before wrapping his sister in a firm, loving embrace that lingered just a moment longer than usual—one of those embraces that said more than words could.

Rachel stepped forward, brushing her hands on her apron as she drew close. She pulled Hila into a warm hug, the scent of flour and herbs still clinging to her.

"Come in, sister," she said, her voice low with welcome. "I just took bread from the oven."

"Good," Hila grinned, glancing toward her children, who were already darting into the courtyard like scattered birds. "Because these ones never stop eating."

The courtyard was alive with the sounds of children playing. Hila's sons and daughters ran in wild, joyful loops beneath the great sycamore, their shrieks of delight rising into the warm afternoon air. Every so often, a small cloud of dust swirled up as they tumbled and rolled, wrestling in the way children always did when left to their own adventures. Their bare feet kicked up the scent of dry earth and the bruised herbs that edged the stone paths—thyme, mint, and wild marjoram crushed beneath their soles.

Abner leaned against the trunk of his tree, arms folded, watching them with a bemused smile. This had become familiar over the years—his sister's visits, her children spilling into his world like a joyful flood, filling the once-quiet spaces with laughter, skinned knees, and endless noise. And yet, he wouldn't trade it.

Nearby, Rachel sat on a woven mat, smoothing her hands over the fabric of her dress as she watched Hila's youngest—a boy with Hila's dark curls and bright, mischievous eyes—stumble toward her, arms outstretched and determined.

Rachel chuckled, steadying him as he collapsed into her lap, nestling eagerly against her side. She wrapped her arms around him without hesitation, drawing him close with a tenderness that came as naturally as breath.

"You're getting far too big for this," she teased softly, brushing a hand over his curls.

The boy looked up at her and grinned, utterly unbothered. "But you give the best cuddles, Doda Hila."

Abner, watching from a short distance, caught the flicker of emotion that crossed Rachel's face. Subtle. Fleeting. But there. A softness. A longing. A quiet ache she never put into words.

She held the boy a moment longer than necessary, her fingers moving gently along his back in slow, absent strokes. Then, as if remembering herself, she loosened her hold, kissed his forehead, and set him back on his feet with a tender smile.

It was not the first time Abner had noticed it.

Rachel never spoke of it—not to him, not to anyone. She was not one to complain, nor did she let sorrow find a voice. But in moments like these, when the house echoed with the laughter of children that were not her own, he saw the silent prayer in her eyes.

A prayer woven from years of waiting.

Hila, sitting a few paces away beneath the shade, saw it too.

"You'd make a wonderful mother, Rachel," Hila murmured, her voice gentle but full of love and deep meaning.

Rachel's lips curved into a soft smile, though her fingers remained lightly curled in her lap, as though still holding onto something unseen. "If the Lord wills it," she said quietly—no bitterness, only quiet trust.

Hila reached for Rachel's hand, giving it a slight squeeze. No more words were needed. In that silence, something sacred passed between them—an understanding that ran deeper than years or circumstance.

From where he stood, Abner swallowed and pushed himself away from the tree. His wife's faith remained unshaken, yet he knew—he *knew*—that beneath her grace and quiet strength, she too had spent years waiting. Hoping.

Just as he had once waited for this very tree to bear its first fruit.

And now, as then, he would trust the timing of the One who gives growth.

The children continued to race through the courtyard, their small feet picking up dust as their laughter echoed through the warm afternoon air. But then, something made them pause.

They stood beneath the great sycamore, their play forgotten as their heads tilted back, gazing up into the thick branches. The leaves shifted and swayed in the windless air, stirred only by the motion of doves nesting high above.

"It's so big," one of them whispered in awe.

Another reached out hesitantly, small fingers pressing against the rough bark. "It never loses its leaves," he murmured. "It always looks the same."

A small voice—one of Hila's younger daughters—broke the quiet. She turned to Abner, wide-eyed and full of innocent wonder.

"Uncle Abner... why?"

Abner inhaled softly, caught off guard by the question. There was no teasing in her voice, no childish mischief—only curiosity, open and sincere.

He had been that child once, standing beneath this very tree, asking that very same question.

But back then, the answer had not been his to give.

Now, it was.

He walked toward them slowly, his gaze lifting to the same branches that had shaded his boyhood and whispered to his manhood. The same tree that had waited—quietly, stubbornly, faithfully—to bear its fruit.

Planted for a purpose

And in that moment, surrounded by innocence and legacy, he began to speak.

He crouched down, meeting her curious gaze. "Because some trees are made to stand through every season." He gestured toward the nearby fig trees, their branches beginning to thin as the colder months settled in. "Some trees let go of their leaves because that's how they were created—to shed, to rest, to wait for new growth. That is how God has planned for them to live."

The children followed his gesture, watching the breeze pluck dried leaves from the fig trees, sending them spiralling toward the ground like tired dancers surrendering to rest.

"But this one..." Abner placed his palm against the sycamore's trunk, feeling its steady strength beneath his touch. "This one was made to endure through every season. To remain."

A hush fell over the children as they absorbed his words, their small hands now pressing gently against the bark as if they, too, were searching for its secret.

Then, one of Hila's older sons let out a gasp. "Look!"

Everyone turned as he pointed upward.

Nestled among the branches, golden in the late light, hung a single ripe fruit—its colour rich, its shape full, kissed by the sun.

Abner's breath caught in his throat.

The first fruit of the season.

It had come slightly early, yet Abner knew—deep in his spirit—that it had ripened at precisely the right time. For this time.

As if the tree itself had been waiting for this moment, offering its quiet reminder.

A reminder of the past.

Of the lessons learned.

Of the blessings still to come.

One of the boys turned to him eagerly, his face alight with wonder. "Can we pick it?"

Abner smiled, shaking his head gently. "Not yet. The first fruit belongs to the Lord."

His eyes drifted toward Hila, who stood watching him from a short distance, her gaze full and knowing.

And in her eyes, he saw it—recognition.

She remembered.

She remembered her father's voice—steady, weathered, sure—teaching them this very truth beneath this very same tree. She remembered Eliab's hands, lined and strong, lifting the first fruit high with reverence, offering it in thanksgiving.

Now, her children would learn.

As she had once learned.

As Abner had once learned.

Abner sat beneath the tree with the children gathered around him, their knees dusted with soil, eyes wide with quiet curiosity. He spoke not as a scholar, but as one passing on something sacred—something lived. He told them of the first offerings of Cain and Abel, and how one gave with reverence while the other gave with reluctance. He spoke of Moses, and how the Lord had given His people a law not to bind them, but to teach them honour, humility, and trust. He explained that the first of anything, the first fruit, the first breath of morning, the first cry of a newborn, belonged to the Lord, as an offering of trust in the rest to come.

And the children listened.

Their attention did not drift, not on this day.

For some reason, they knew they were hearing more than a story.

Planted for a purpose

They were being given something ancient. Something alive.

And so, the faithfulness of God would be carried forward, one season at a time.

As the sun began to set, the adults sat together beneath the sycamore tree, watching the children play in the fading golden light. The laughter of the little ones mixed with the distant hum of the evening wind, weaving through the courtyard like a melody long familiar yet ever new.

Rachel poured wine into their cups, the rich aroma mingling with the scent of the earth still warm from the day's heat. Her movements were gentle, almost ceremonial—hands steady, eyes calm. Hila passed around small bowls of dried figs and almonds, her hands moving with the practised ease of a mother who always ensured others were cared for before herself. She knew what each child liked, how many almonds Abner would take without asking, and when Rachel needed an extra moment of stillness.

"I was thinking of Ima today," Hila murmured, her voice soft, almost lost to the breeze.

Abner lifted his gaze from his cup, his fingers tightening slightly around the clay. The mention of their mother stirred something rooted and tender. He didn't speak right away—didn't need to. The silence between them bore the shape of her memory.

"I think of her often, too," Rachel said, not interrupting Hila's story, but gently entering the sacred circle of daughtership they both shared. Her voice was warm with affection, though a trace of longing lingered just beneath the surface. Naamah had loved them both fiercely—had taken Rachel into her heart not as a duty, but as a joy. From the moment of her wedding to Abner, she had called her not only daughter-in-law, but *daughter*.

"She would have loved to see them all together like this," Hila added, her voice softening as her eyes followed the children in their dance of freedom—unburdened, laughing, alive. "She used to say it was her favourite sound. The sound of children who feel safe."

Rachel nodded, smiling gently. "She would have sat right here with us, watching every little thing, remembering every little moment, retelling it later with more detail than anyone thought possible."

"She would have joined them," Abner added with a wistful chuckle, glancing toward the children as if expecting to see her among them, skirts swishing, laughter rising. "And Abba would have been sitting right here, telling stories none of them understood yet."

"Just like you've done a few times, too, Abner?" Rachel teased, resting her hand lovingly on her husband's shoulder.

A quiet laugh rippled through the group, but then the moment deepened—the absence settling in alongside the presence.

Though Naamah's voice no longer filled the courtyard, her memory lingered in every corner. In the way Hila mothered. In the way Rachel welcomed. In the way Abner listened before he spoke.

She was gone from their sight—but not from the story.

Not from *this* story.

Somewhere, a bird called from the branches above them, its song low and sweet—mellow, unhurried, the kind of sound that fills a silence without needing to break it.

Hila turned toward Abner, her voice softer now, as if drawn from the quiet itself. "Do you think they would be proud of us?"

Abner didn't answer right away.

Instead, he looked up at the sycamore tree—its broad arms stretching heavenward, the leaves whispering memories only they could hear. How many times had he stood beneath this tree, longing

| *Planted for a purpose*

for answers? And how often had he heard nothing but wind?

Now, he didn't need to ask.

A slow breath filled his lungs. His mother had once told him, *"One day, you'll know when to speak. You'll feel it—not in your head, but here."* She had pressed his hand to his chest. *"Like your Abba does."*

And now, without searching, without striving, the words came—quiet and sure, already written in the grain of who he had become.

"They already were."

Hila's eyes glistened. She pressed her lips together, nodding, the weight and wonder of his words resting between them like a blessing.

Beside him, Rachel reached for Abner's hand. Her fingers were warm, confident, familiar. He looked at her—the woman who had become his home—and he knew.

Though the seasons had changed, and time had moved on, the past had never left them.

It was here.

Woven into the laughter of children.

Into the love that remained.

Into the tree that still stood—steadfast, unshaken, the keeper of memory and meaning.

As the evening deepened, the children eventually settled around Abner, their boundless energy giving way to quiet curiosity. One of them leaned against his knee, gazing up at him with wide, wondering eyes.

"Dod Abner," the child asked, small fingers tracing absent patterns in the dust, "does your tree have a name?"

Abner blinked, caught off guard by the question. A name?

For many years, it had simply been *the tree*—a quiet presence, a witness, a companion. It had grown as he had grown. It had weathered storms, welcomed seasons, and waited in silence. It had never asked to be seen, yet somehow was always noticed. Faithful. Constant. Always there.

Now, standing here with the next generation watching and learning, it seemed only right.

He glanced at Hila, at Rachel, at the children gathered close, eyes wide with anticipation. The kind of question that didn't need to be asked twice.

A slow smile formed on his lips.

"*Emunah,*" he said at last.

The children whispered the name among themselves, testing it, tasting it. A soft murmur of wonder passed between them, like wind through leaves.

"What does it mean?" one of them asked, his voice almost reverent.

Abner's eyes returned to the tree—its branches still outstretched toward heaven, its roots deep in soil that had known both sorrow and song.

Hila and Rachel answered at the same time, their voices warm—soft as a whisper, united as family.

"Faithfulness."

A gentle breeze stirred the branches above them, rustling the leaves with a sound like a quiet *amen*.

And beneath the canopy of the tree—beneath *Emunah*—they sat together, a family bound not only by love, but by the faithfulness that had carried them through every season.

Chapter Fifteen:
The Empty Chair

The air in the house was oppressively heavy.

It was strange—so full, and yet so empty. The woven chairs remained in their place. The jars of flour and oil sat undisturbed on the shelf. The linen was still folded neatly in the corner.

And yet, everywhere Abner looked, there was absence. Even the familiar creak of the shutters in the morning breeze had fallen silent. Light filtered in through the wooden slats, stretching across the floor in soft, pale ribbons—gentle reminders of a world still moving outside.

He could hear the distant sounds of the town beginning to stir—merchants setting up their stalls, donkeys braying, the rhythmic clatter of pots and vessels—but inside this house, their house, there was only quiet.

The kind of quiet that follows the greatest of loss.

The kind that settles not only over a place, but within a soul.

Rachel had passed in the early hours before dawn. She had been unwell for many weeks, her strength slowly ebbing like the final drops of oil in a flickering lamp. She was not old—not truly by the years Abner had counted for himself. But her body had grown weary, and her time had come.

And her spirit had left peacefully, without distress.

She had known it. She had said as much, with a soft voice and calm eyes.

"I have been given so much," she had whispered the night before, her fingers tracing the lines of his hand as though memorising them one last time.

"And though I never held a child of my own, I have never been empty. Abner, because of you, my life has been so full—more love than I ever thought I could hold."

Abner had wept quietly at her words, his forehead resting against hers.

"You filled my life, Rachel. More than you'll ever know. Thank you for loving me, for choosing me, for being my beautiful wife—my love."

His voice had trembled with sorrow, laced with the unspoken fear that these might be the last words she would ever hear.

They had spoken often in the long weeks of her illness—always words of love and gratitude for what they had shared, for the life they had built together. Words of trust in the Lord's faithfulness through every joy and every sorrow.

They had spoken, too, of the disappointments. The silent prayers. The unanswered hopes that had long since been laid to rest.

And yet, never once had Rachel called herself forgotten. Never once had she allowed grief to steal her peace.

"Like Hannah," she had said, not long before her final night. "Hannah wept. She prayed. But even before the Lord opened her womb, she had already given herself to Him. She was never empty."

Rachel had smiled then—softly, steadily—her voice calm as still waters.

"And neither was I. I may not have received what I longed for... but God gave me all I needed. And in that, more than I ever dreamed."

Abner remembered the way her lips had curved into that same gentle smile—the one that had first caught his breath the night of

Hila's wedding.

It had never faded. Not even in the hardest years.

He saw that smile one last time.

And then, like a candle that chooses its own moment to extinguish, she slipped from this world with peace written across her face, her hand still resting in his.

Now, in the quiet hours of the morning, Abner remained where he had been for hours.

The woven chair beside him—*hers*—sat empty. A shawl still draped across its back, as though she had only just stepped away.

The bread she had half-kneaded the day before still sat covered near the hearth.

Her jar of spices remained neatly arranged, untouched.

Every part of the house felt paused, not abandoned. Not yet.

Abner closed his eyes and pressed his palm to his chest.

The ache was not loud.

It was not the sharp, searing grief he had known when Eliab passed.

Nor the dull, slow ache that had followed Naamah.

This was different.

Deeper. Quieter. Like a well dug so far into the earth its waters could not be seen—and yet, he knew they were there. He rose slowly, his bones stiff with the weight of years, and stepped outside.

The courtyard was bathed in morning light, soft and golden, like a memory he could walk through but not touch. And there, standing as it always had, was the tree.

Emunah.

Abner moved toward it, his sandals brushing the dust with each step.

Planted for a purpose

He placed a hand on its bark—rough, solid beneath his fingers—and looked up into its branches.

So many of his loved ones had placed their hands on this tree.

It had stood as a silent witness through the years—through joy and sorrow, through love and loss.

And through all that time, it had never once stopped growing.

It had endured storms, droughts, seasons of abundance, and seasons of waiting.

It had borne fruit and stood bare, and still it had endured.

Just like Rachel.

His beautiful Rachel.

She had never let sorrow shape her.

She had never let bitterness take root.

Even in her longing, she had chosen joy.

Even in her barrenness, she had known her life was full.

Even in her final moments, she had trusted—truly trusted—that God had been enough.

A woman of faithfulness.

A woman of *emunah*.

He sat beneath the tree, in the chair he had carved with her name. *Rachel.*

His eyes drifted shut as he exhaled a long, unsteady breath.

It felt too heavy to hold.

"How, God?"

Not *why*—he had long made peace with the mystery of why—but how.

"How am I to go on? How, when the one You gave me has been taken away too soon... *how*?"

Tears slid down his weathered cheeks, hot and steady.

And then the sobs came—deep and raw—wracking his ageing frame, as if something ancient had broken loose within him.

And the tree stood still, its branches stretching toward heaven, bearing witness once more.

The prayer wasn't spoken aloud.

It rose from somewhere deeper than words— from the hollow places within him that had no language left— and it lingered there, suspended in the hush like incense rising from a hidden altar, waiting for a response only heaven could give.

Abner remembered his *Ima* once telling him, when he was still a boy, that there were prayers which needed to be asked— but that some answers required no words at all. "You must learn to listen," she had said, brushing dust from his cheek with her calloused fingers. "Not just with your ears, but with your spirit."

Now, sitting beneath the branches of *Emunah*, he wasn't even sure what the question should be.

But still, he listened.

The other chair beside him bore his own name— *Abner*— carved gently into the back, its edges worn smooth by time and weather. But today, that seat was not for him. Today, he needed to be close to *her*. He reached into his pocket and drew out the cloth Rachel had embroidered— its edges softened from years of use, a single sycamore leaf stitched in the corner with neat, careful hands.

He laid it gently across her chair, smoothing it slowly, deliberately— a sacred act, small and tender, yet weighty with meaning.

An offering of presence.

Of remembrance.

Of love that still remained.

Above him, the breeze stirred with a hush, brushing through the branches like fingers across harp strings. Leaves rustled overhead, and for a fleeting moment, he could almost hear her laughter again—light, warm, echoing softly between the branches like the last note of a song still lingering in the air.

And then, so gently he almost missed it, he felt it.

A whisper.

"You have sacrificed much for Me."

The words did not come with thunder.

They did not shake the earth or burn within his bones.

They came as a breath.

As a memory.

As oil poured into an empty vessel.

"You've been faithful, Abner. Let Me show you My faithfulness again."

Abner's shoulders dropped. His eyes brimmed, and for a moment, the weight of silence felt almost bearable. His heart stirred, reaching backwards through memory, recalling a story, one not often told aloud, but buried deep in the scriptures of his youth.

The prophet Elijah—alone, exhausted, pressed by fear—had once hidden himself in a cave. He had fled, broken and afraid, believing he had failed, that all he had done for the Lord had come to nothing.

He had expected God to come in fire. In thunder. In wind.

But the Lord came in none of those.

He came in the stillness. In the whisper.

And it was there, in that hushed moment, that Elijah heard the truth—not only of who God was, but of who he still was... and who he was still called to be.

Abner's breath caught in his chest. He could almost hear his father's voice—steady, tender—beneath this very tree, telling that story on a warm evening many years ago.

"No, Abner... just listen."

And so, he did.

Abner rested. His eyes closed, his hands relaxed in his lap, and for a long while, he allowed the still, small voice of God to speak—not to his ears, but to his spirit.

There were no words.

No audible sounds.

Just stillness.

Shared between an old man and his Father.

The One who had always been there.

Who would never leave him.

Never forsake him.

When Abner woke in the early afternoon, the courtyard had not changed.

The same shadows danced beneath the tree. The same breeze rustled the leaves. The same ache pulsed gently in his chest.

He was still without his Rachel. He was still grieving.

And yet—though he could not yet shape the question buried in the deepest part of his soul—he knew...

He already had the answer.

Not gone. Just gone ahead.

He leaned back and closed his eyes. The tree would keep standing.

And so would he.

A little bent.

A little weathered.

But still faithful.

Still rooted.

Still enduring.

Like her.

Chapter Sixteen:
Beneath the Branches

The mid-morning sun filtered gently through the leaves of the sycamore tree, scattering patterns of golden light that danced across the dusty courtyard. A warm breeze stirred the branches overhead, carrying with it the faint scent of dry earth and jasmine. The tree—ancient now—stood as tall and strong as ever, its roots buried deep in the soil, its branches stretching wide, as if holding the memories of a lifetime beneath its shade.

Abner sat quietly in his chair beneath the tree, his hands folded loosely in his lap, his shoulders more stooped than they once were. His hair had long since turned silver, and his skin was etched with the lines of years well lived. And yet his eyes—dark and sharp—still sparkled with the wisdom of age and the weight of memory. His tunic, simple and well-worn, fluttered slightly in the breeze, and the soles of his sandals rested just within the dappled light, touching both sun and shadow.

Two of Hila's adult children approached from the path, their steps slow and careful as they guided their mother forward. Hila leaned gently on their arms. Her frame, smaller now with age, still carried the quiet dignity that had always defined her. Her hair, mostly grey, was plaited neatly down her back. Her eyes—so like their mother's, so like her brother's—still shone with mischief and strength, undimmed by the years.

"Here we are, Ima," one of her sons murmured, steadying her as she lowered herself into the carved wooden chair beside Abner. Abner smiled up at them, remembering the many times when these very boys had been small, how they would rush at him with loving arms open, squealing with joy and laughter.

Abner chuckled to himself, quietly relieved that the boys, now grown men, had well outgrown that type of greeting for him.

Hila's hand brushed over the arm of the chair instinctively, her fingers trailing the worn wood, though she did not yet notice the detail etched there. She breathed heavily, worn from the walk and the effort it had taken to cross the courtyard.

Abner looked over at her with a soft smile. "You made it, little sister."

"I told you I would," she replied, her voice still strong despite the gentle tremble beneath it. "Though I'm not as quick as I once was."

Abner chuckled. "None of us are."

They sat in companionable silence for a while, the breeze rustling the leaves above them, the sounds of the town drifting faintly in the distance. Children's laughter rang out softly from somewhere beyond the courtyard wall. The occasional bray of a donkey or the distant clang of pottery being stacked reminded them that life still moved forward, even as they sat in its quieter pause.

"It's all still the same," Hila said at last, her eyes taking in the courtyard before lifting slowly to the canopy of the tree.

"Only taller," Abner replied. "Like the rest of us were meant to be."

A smile crept onto her face. "Except I never quite caught up to you."

He gave a low laugh. "You caught up in all the ways that mattered."

They were quiet again for a while, letting the breeze fill the spaces between their thoughts, until Hila's voice returned—softer now, woven with memory.

"I miss him."

Abner turned toward her. "Your husband?"

She nodded. "He was good to me, Abner. Patient. Strong. We didn't always agree on everything, but he never let a day end without *shalom* between us."

"I always respected him," Abner said. "Even when he couldn't keep up with your wit. He tried, even though his efforts were futile." He smiled, a touch of mischief warming his expression. "You were always the one who could calm any storm."

Hila chuckled softly, her hand brushing his arm with familiar affection. "I miss Rachel so very much, too." Her eyes lingered on the courtyard, as though expecting to see Rachel's figure emerging from the kitchen with a smile, wiping her hands on her apron.

Abner nodded, his voice quiet. "She loved you like a sister, Hila." He turned slightly toward her. "She always said you were the sister she had always wanted—the one her heart had chosen, not just her family."

Hila's breath caught slightly, and she blinked hard. "I know," she said, her voice faltering with the weight of memory. "And she... she was never bitter, Abner. Never jealous. Never angry with God. Even when her prayers went unanswered—at least in the way she once hoped—they never hardened her. She carried sorrow, yes... but never let it become her identity."

She paused, her gaze lifting to the leaves above them. "She loved so fully, especially my children. From the moment they were born, she treated them as if they were her own, without hesitation. She never made me feel guilty for what I had that she didn't. In fact, she rejoiced with me many times. And the boys... they adored her. Still do. She wasn't just my friend or their 'aunt.' She was their second mother and my sister."

Abner's eyes glistened, and he lowered his head slightly. "She filled every room she entered," he murmured. "Laughter followed her like a fragrance. Even now, I feel her here... not like a memory, but as if she's just stepped out for a moment and will return any second."

"I do too," Hila whispered. "Even though Rachel didn't grow up here with us... she became part of what made this place—this tree, this home—what it is. Without her, the roots would still be strong... but the branches wouldn't have stretched so wide."

They sat for a long time beneath the dappled light, their words weaving through the still air like threads of memory. They spoke of their childhood—of the time Abner had fallen from the neighbour's fig tree and broken his arm, stubbornly refusing to cry until he saw Naamah's tears spilling silently down her cheeks. He had cried then, not from pain, but from the sight of her sorrow.

And of Hila, who used to sneak wrapped sweets in the folds of her shawl during Sukkot, quietly passing them into the small hands of children too shy—or too well-mannered—to ask for more. Her eyes twinkled at the memory, and Abner could almost see her younger self again, eyes mischievous but heart wide open.

They chuckled together over the memory of Eliab's booming voice echoing through the courtyard like a trumpet blast, summoning Abner to help stack firewood. But more often than not, the task would be abandoned halfway through as Eliab launched into one of his long, winding stories—his eyes alight, his hands gesturing wildly—while Abner listened, utterly spellbound.

And always, there was Naamah—the gentle heart of the home. Forever near the hearth, her hands kneading or stirring or folding, her back bowed but her spirit never weary. She had hummed lullabies without ceasing, the melodies soft and lilting, wrapping the household in comfort like a well-worn blanket. She was music, even in silence.

Abner smiled faintly. "She used to sing that one song—what was it? The one about the fig tree and the sparrow?"

Hila's eyes lit up with recognition. "Yes," she said, her voice touched with delight. "'Even the sparrow finds a home.' She said it reminded her of this courtyard. Of this very tree."

Abner's eyes grew distant with memory. "She also said the same thing when she first met Rachel," he added softly. "That Rachel had found her home here. I think... I think that was the moment Rachel truly felt she belonged—not just to me, but to all of us. And of course, it could only have been Ima who said the right thing at the right time. She always knew."

Hila nodded, the tears in her eyes catching the light like morning dew. "You gave each other something beautiful."

A long silence followed, gentle and unhurried. The kind that rests comfortably between old friends.

"My children grew up hearing their stories," Hila said eventually, her voice quiet and contemplative. "I wanted them to know where they came from. What kind of childhood we had—and the kind of love that built this family."

"You told them about the tree?" Abner asked, glancing up at the thick canopy above them. Its branches still held the laughter, the tears, the prayers of all who had come before.

"I told them everything," she replied. "About the waiting. About the first fruit. About how you wouldn't let Barak forget what he did." A soft chuckle escaped her lips. "But mostly, I told them about you, Abner."

She turned to him, her voice tender. "I told them how you never stopped believing, how you planted something even when it made no sense to hope, how you stayed when others would have run. And how you loved—not just Rachel—but all of us. As if it were the most natural thing in the world."

Abner looked down, blinking against the sudden sting in his eyes. His throat tightened, but he did not speak. He didn't need to.

The tree rustled above them, a breeze threading through its leaves like a quiet amen.

He looked at her, puzzled by the weight in her voice. But Hila didn't look away. Instead, she leaned forward slightly, her hands resting on her knees, her eyes locked with his.

"You were never just my brother, Abner," she said quietly. "You were my safe place. My shelter. When everything else in our world shifted, you remained steady. Like you once told me—some trees are made to stand through every season."

Abner's breath caught. His mouth opened slightly, but for a moment, no words came. Then he lowered his gaze, blinking against the warmth pressing behind his eyes.

"I only stood," he said slowly, "because of what Abba and Ima poured into us. Their prayers. Their teaching. Their love." He paused, then looked back at her. "And because you never let me fall. Even when I wanted to."

Hila smiled softly, her gaze filled with quiet pride.

"My sons," she said after a moment, "they are the men they are today not only because of their father, but because of you. Because of what they saw in you. Strength, patience, faith. They learned that from their uncle. From the man who carved chairs not just with names, but with love."

A breeze stirred between them, rustling the canopy above. The branches swayed with the wind, and the golden light shifted, dancing across their faces, gentle and unhurried. It felt like a breath from Heaven—a benediction.

Hila tilted her head slightly, her voice soft. "Do you remember, Abner... how Ima used to say that blessing every time we left the house?"

Abner gave a slow, reverent nod. "Every time," he echoed. "Even when we were grown."

They looked at each other, and then, as if drawn by some deep, familiar pull, their voices lifted together. Frail with age, but steady with memory—spoken like a sacred inheritance:

"May the Lord bless you and keep you.

May He make His face shine upon you and be gracious to you.

May He lift up His countenance upon you,

And give you peace."

The words hung in the air like the hush after a psalm. Not an ending. A benediction over all that had been—and all that still remained.

The words settled over them like sunlight through leaves—ancient, familiar, sacred.

"They'll carry it forward," Abner said softly. "Just like we did."

Hila gave a slow nod, her eyes glistening. "I believe they will. They've seen enough of what matters to know what to keep."

And so they remained—talking, remembering, pausing often

between stories to let the silence speak. The silence that wasn't empty, but full of the weight of years, of echoes and prayers and faces now gone.

They laughed gently over childhood mischief, marvelled at how the years had passed so swiftly, and spoke of their parents with a reverence that had only deepened over time. And then they simply sat. No longer needing words. Content in the kind of presence that only family, and only time, could forge.

As the early afternoon wore on, the sun dipped lower, stretching long shadows across the courtyard like a soft cloak. The air grew warmer, still, quieter.

Hila's children returned from beyond the gate, their voices hushed as they stepped closer. One of her sons knelt beside her, brushing the dust from her hem.

"Ima, are you ready to go?"

She looked toward Abner, her expression thoughtful, then slowly rose to her feet. Her body protested, but her spirit remained strong.

Not letting go of the moment, she reached out and clasped Abner's hands, firm, both to steady herself and to linger just a little longer.

"I don't know how many more times we'll sit like this," she whispered, her voice trembling but resolute.

Abner held her gaze, his grip firm, eyes soft. "Then we make this one count," he replied.

And in that moment, they did.

She held him in a long embrace, breathing in the moment. Their foreheads touched briefly—a gesture that echoed both the simplicity of childhood affection and the quiet strength of adult solidarity.

As she turned to leave, her hand brushed the arm of her chair once more.

And then she saw it.

Her name.

Engraved beside the grain, weathered but clear:

Hila

She paused, her fingers tracing it softly.

Her eyes shimmered. "You always were sentimental."

Abner shrugged, a half-smile playing at his lips. "Only for the ones I couldn't live without."

She bent, kissed his cheek, and gave his hand one last squeeze.

He didn't let go right away.

There, in the quiet weight of their clasped hands, was everything:

Memories.

Family.

Love.

And then, leaning on her children, she turned and walked away—each step slow, steady, and sure.

Abner remained beneath the tree, watching until they disappeared down the path. The breeze whispered softly through the leaves, and the shadows stretched farther across the courtyard.

The chair beside him sat empty.

But not alone.

Chapter Seventeen:
The Visitor

The light of early afternoon glistened across the courtyard, slanting golden through the branches of the great sycamore tree. Its broad canopy swayed gently in the breeze, casting shifting shadows across the familiar space beneath. The tree had stood through every season—through every joy, every sorrow. And today, as on so many days, Abner sat beneath it—his carved wooden chair cradling him like an old friend's embrace.

His eyes, though dulled with age, still held their quiet spark. He was older now than anyone in his family had ever been. His hands, once firm and capable, rested gently in his lap, their contours slightly curled with time and wear. Yet his posture remained peaceful. Steady. Watching. A blanket was draped across his frail legs, lending warmth and comfort to a frame now worn and waning. Beside him, a small clay cup of water sat untouched, catching the last glow of the sun as it dipped lower in the sky.

There had been murmurs all through the town since morning—an energy that shimmered on the air like the hum of bees in early spring. A prophet was passing through Jericho. But not just any prophet, they said. This was the one from Galilee. The one who taught with authority, who healed the sick, and who forgave sins. Some called Him Rabbi. Others whispered... ha-Mashiach, *Messiah*.

Abner had heard the talk. He had even listened with quiet interest as the younger ones repeated stories of blind men who now saw, of storms calmed with a word, of lepers restored and hearts made whole. They spoke of hope. Of change. Of something eternal breaking into the ordinary.

But Abner was tired now. He had walked many seasons. His body ached, and his soul, though full, was nearing its rest. He had no strength for crowds. No desire to push through noise and clamour to catch a glimpse of a stranger, no matter how wondrous.

"This is for the young ones," he had murmured to himself. "What use has a prophet for an old man like me?"

And yet, as the sun dipped lower behind the rooftops, a sound began to rise in the distance—soft at first, but growing.

It drifted toward him like the murmur of an approaching storm, not fierce or threatening, but full of energy. From somewhere down the dusty road, voices stirred—shouting, laughing, overlapping in waves of joy and confusion. The rhythm of hurried footsteps beat against the earth. Children's cries of delight rang out ahead of the throng, their bare feet slapping the path as they darted forward, untethered and gleeful. Mothers called after them, their voices swept up in the swell. Even the steady calls of merchants hawking goods had fallen silent, their stalls left behind as heads turned and hearts leapt.

Something, or someone, was coming.

The noise gathered, like wind collecting itself before it changes the air. It rolled up the road and around the bend, pulling more bodies into its wake with each passing moment.

And then... it swelled.

A tide of sound and movement.

The crowd was not just nearby.

The crowd was coming *this* way.

Abner shifted in his chair, slow and careful. His joints protested, but he straightened all the same, lifting his gaze toward the bend in the road. The path that curved along the edge of his courtyard had often seen friends, neighbours, even the occasional traveller pass by. But this was no ordinary passing.

He could hear them now—clearly, unmistakably.

Voices crying out with desperate hope. Others were calling His name again and again. Questions shouted. Pleas lifted high and rising in volume and intensity. Woven through it all, the unmistakable sound of rejoicing.

The prophet was near.

And they were coming right past his tree.

And at the front of it all—slipping through gaps, darting left and right like a man both frantic and focused—was someone Abner recognised.

The town's tax collector.

Zacchaeus.

Abner's brows furrowed. "Of all the people," he muttered to himself.

Zacchaeus was not a man known for humility or popularity. He was small in stature, but never missed. Quick-footed, sharp-eyed, and cloaked in a shrewdness that left most people muttering under their breath the moment he passed. His name, when spoken, usually came with a sneer.

But now... he looked entirely different.

There was no smugness. No measured pride.

Only desperation.

Abner watched as the man leapt futilely to glimpse over the shoulders of the taller crowd. He tiptoed, pivoted, craned his neck.

| *Planted for a purpose*

He ducked between strangers, was shoved aside, circled back, then dashed forward again, scanning the growing mass of bodies with the wide-eyed urgency of someone drowning—searching for a rope. A breath. A way through.

Then his eyes landed on the tree.

And on the old man sitting on the chair beneath it.

Their eyes met—Abner's steady and calm, Zacchaeus's wild and pleading.

For the briefest of moments, time seemed to hesitate.

Abner gave the slightest nod. A knowing gesture, as if to say: *Go ahead. You're not the first.*

Without hesitation, Zacchaeus moved.

He rushed forward, his fingers gripping the trunk with the confidence of one who had climbed trees in his youth but not for many years. His feet searched the familiar footholds, worn smooth by decades of children and family, by memory. And then, with a surprising burst of agility, he pulled himself into the lower branches, steadying his weight, his breath ragged, his eyes scanning the path ahead.

He perched there, tense, expectant, utterly absorbed.

And then the crowd shifted.

From within the throng, a figure stepped forward.

There was no need to ask who He was.

Abner's breath caught—sharp and sudden.

He didn't understand why.

But something stirred.

Deep.

Wordless.

A whisper in his soul that had no origin... and yet felt older than breath itself.

The man was not tall. Not imposing. His presence did not demand attention—yet it commanded it all the same.

There was a stillness about him. A gravity that did not press, but invited. The very air around him seemed to yield as he passed, as though creation itself knew Him and deferred to His steps. His gait was calm, deliberate, unhurried. And his face... it bore the marks of both joy and deep sorrow. Laughter lines etched by compassion, and furrows that hinted at griefs carried in silence. He was ageless—and yet more human than anyone Abner had ever seen.

And then there were his eyes.

Abner could not look away.

They were not the eyes of a man casually observing a crowd. They were searching, yes—but not uncertain. As if He already knew every face, every story. As if He had known them all before time had given them breath. There was no judgment in them. No fear. Only... truth. And mercy. And something more ancient still—something like love wrapped in glory.

And then, He stopped.

Right beneath the sycamore tree.

Beneath Emunah.

He looked up.

His gaze found Zacchaeus instantly—unmistakably.

And in that moment, everything stilled.

The crowd hushed, confused.

Zacchaeus froze where he perched, clinging to the branch like a child caught doing something he wasn't supposed to.

Planted for a purpose

And then the Man smiled.

A smile that held no mockery, no scorn. Only invitation. Only welcome.

"Zacchaeus."

Just his name. But it rang with purpose. With knowing.

The tax collector's breath hitched.

Then came the words:

"Hurry and come down, for today I must stay at your house."

Gasps rippled through the crowd, whispers like thunder.

"Sinner."

"Outcast."

"Traitor."

The words hissed through clenched teeth and furrowed brows—shock veiled in piety, offence cloaked in righteousness.

But Jesus was not deterred.

He didn't flinch. He didn't turn to explain. His eyes remained on Zacchaeus—steady, unwavering, sure.

Zacchaeus stumbled from the branches, catching his foot as he dropped down, landing hard on both feet with a grunt. Dust rose around him. He wavered slightly, breathless, eyes wide with a mix of awe and disbelief. For a heartbeat, he didn't speak—only looked up into the face of the One who had just called him by name.

Jesus.

The crowd leaned in, the buzz of speculation thinning into a taut, expectant hush. The same people who once parted from Zacchaeus in disdain now stood motionless, held captive by the weight of the moment.

"If..." Zacchaeus began, voice cracked and trembling. He swallowed and tried again.

"If I have wronged anyone…" He stopped, glanced quickly over his shoulder, meeting the eyes of a merchant he had once overcharged, of a widow he had dismissed with a sneer. His shoulders heaved, his shame laid bare.

"If I have wronged anyone," he repeated, louder now, clearer, "I will repay them. Four times over."

A gasp rose in response, but he was not finished.

"I give—" his voice wavered again, but he pressed on. "Half. Half of everything I have… I give to the poor."

He looked at Jesus then. Not for approval. Not even for pity. But because he could no longer look anywhere else. Jesus held his gaze, not with scrutiny, but with tenderness so fierce it seemed to wrap around Zacchaeus like a cloak. Then the Rabbi—this Man from Galilee, dusty from travel yet wrapped in holy authority—nodded.

And spoke.

"Today…" His voice was strong, clear, and it rang out as if for heaven itself to hear. "Today, salvation has come to this house."

A wave of murmurs swept through the crowd, startled and hushed. But Jesus was not finished.

"For the Son of Man has come to seek and to save that which was lost."

The words settled like rain after drought. The crowd, uncertain whether to cheer or tremble, fell still. The self-righteous stood silent. The forgotten looked on with new hope. And Zacchaeus… Zacchaeus wept.

Then Jesus turned. He looked at the tree again, and His gaze found Abner. Their eyes met. Just for a moment. But in that moment, time stood still. Abner felt it—like the first warmth of sunlight after a long winter.

Planted for a purpose

Those eyes.
Abner had seen eyes like that before.
At the planting of a tree.
At the side of a dying wife.
In the laughter of his sister.
In the wisdom of his father.
In the songs of his mother.
They were the eyes of the Creator.
Jesus stepped forward.
He leaned in slightly, his voice low, tender, meant only for Abner.
"Emunah."
Faithfulness.
A word.
A name.
A life.
Abner closed his eyes.
The breeze stirred again, warm and gentle.
His hands relaxed in his lap.
His chest rose and fell.
Slowly.
Evenly.
Softly.
The courtyard settled into sacred stillness.
The tree above him swayed.
The shadows lengthened.
And the chair beside him—marked with a name and a memory—sat empty.
But not alone.
Abner was home.

Acknowledgements

Every story has roots, and this one grew from a place of quiet prompting and steady obedience. I could not have brought it to life without the generosity, wisdom, and faithfulness of others.

To Kimberly Mary, my editor and now cherished creative companion, thank you for journeying with me once again. It was a privilege to work with you again. From It Was His Eyes to Planted for a Purpose, your discernment and dedication continue to refine my words without ever silencing their heart. You see what the story is becoming long before I do, and I am grateful beyond words.

To my cover designer, thank you for bringing this story to life with dignity and beauty through your vision and care. You gave the novel its first voice—visually—before the first page was ever turned.

Thank you to my amazing typesetter, Judy Sery from Sparrow Publishing Agency, for taking the heart of the text and shaping it with such care and artistry—your dedication brought these pages to life with beauty and clarity.

To those who read the early drafts, offered thoughts, or cheered from the sidelines—thank you. Your encouragement whispered "keep going" when I needed it most.

To my family, once again, a massive thank you for making room for this calling. For every quiet hour, every paused conversation, and every nod of belief, you made space for the story to grow.

To the teachers, pastors, and storytellers whose voices shaped my own, your influence is written on every page. You taught me how to

Planted for a purpose

listen for God's voice within the narrative.

And above all, to the Author of life—the One who plants, prunes, and brings purpose out of every season: may every word bring You honour. This story, like all others I write, is for You.

About the Author

Craig Minty is a teacher, storyteller, and lifelong student of Scripture. With over 25 years of experience in many schools and Christian education, he has taught generations of students to think deeply, live purposefully, and recognise the redemptive thread woven throughout the Bible.

Craig holds degrees in Music, Education, and Theology, and has served in various leadership roles across primary and secondary schools in Australia. His passion for biblical narrative, spiritual symbolism, and character-driven fiction is at the heart of his writing.

His debut novel, *It Was His Eyes*, invites readers into a first-century world of betrayal, forgiveness, and the transforming power of Jesus' gaze. His second book, *Planted for a Purpose*, continues his mission to tell stories that are both theologically rich and emotionally resonant.

In addition to his fiction work, Craig is currently developing *The Four C's: A Relational Teaching Model for the Secondary School*—a framework designed to support educators in building meaningful, growth-oriented relationships with students.

He lives in Melbourne, Australia, with his wife Caroline. When not writing, teaching, or playing piano, he enjoys long drives, strong coffee, and time spent bushwalking among trees that whisper stories of their own.

Follow Craig's journey and future releases at:

@savedbygracestories

Other Books by the Author

It Was His Eyes — A first-century tale of failure, forgiveness, and the love that transforms us.

Planted for a Purpose — A story of growth, identity, and God's quiet, redemptive work across a lifetime.

To follow Craig's future releases, visit: **@savedbygracestories**

Before You Go...

If this story spoke to you—if it encouraged your faith, stirred something deep within, or reminded you that your life is planted with purpose—would you consider leaving a short review?

Your words don't need to be long or polished. Just a sentence or two can help someone else discover this story and be reminded that God sees them... and hasn't forgotten their purpose either.

You can leave a review wherever you purchased the book, or share your thoughts on Instagram by tagging: **@savedbygracestories**

Thank you for reading—and thank you for helping this story take root in new hearts.

Made in United States
Cleveland, OH
15 November 2025